The Keys to the Riad

CD DAMITIO

WHITNEY MORGAN

The Keys to the Riad

Cover art and Illustrations

made by the Publisher

with the assistance of Midjourney

ISBN: 978-1-962668-05-7

For my daughter Sophia, a powerful Moroccan woman in the making.

The most powerful women are the ones who are really in charge, men rarely figure this out. Don't tell!

The Keys to the Riad

TABLE OF CONTENTS

The Ring of Fools

Chapter 1: The Ring of Fools

Hot sweat sizzled down her forehead, attacking her eyebrows before making the victorious plunge into her eyes. The salt stung, but she tried to ignore it and keep her vision clear because the consequences of a moment of distraction were too high to allow. A split second of attention loss would put her face down, bloody, and bruised. Victories are created, not by heroic acts of larger-than-life valor, but instead by overcoming the things that most people never even notice.

It was the story of her life. The story of her lifestyle. The story of her lifeless corpse twitching at the end of a rope. She was the 'it' girl. The woman everyone wanted to be. Jokingly referred to by her friends as 'The Great'. Those around her saw clearly that she was in control. She was in control of everything but her own destiny. If they had thought of it, the girls in her school would have voted her 'Most likely to have everything.'

She was popular, charming, and beautiful. More importantly and possibly because she felt like she had to prove to herself that she actually deserved the success she enjoyed, she worked harder, fought longer, and refused to ever give up. The finish line was just a starting point for her, and she was known for crossing it and refusing to stop. She was focused, driven, and as tough as a cast iron frying pan.

And yet, her life felt like it was missing something. She didn't know what was missing. It was something just out of reach, just around the bend, just over the horizon. Her pragmatism told her that destiny was a fool's devotion, but sometimes she would board trains without a destination in mind, hoping beyond hope that she might be led to that which she was missing.

The stinging in her eyes was too much, and despite a Herculean effort to not do it, her gloved hand reached up to wipe it from her vision. For the barest of moments, her attention was distracted as the glove pushed a thick strand of golden-brown hair in front of her face. There was no room for distraction.

She caught sight of a red bomb hurtling towards her from the right side, a peripheral moment of clarity coming a bare instant before the unbearable pain. Her hands were in the wrong place to block, her stance made it impossible for her to dodge, and the screaming haymaker knocked her back against the ropes and opened her up to an unbelievably rapid series of body blows that culminated in a powerful uppercut that sent her up, flat, and on her ass - the hard way.

Her mind screamed orders at her defeated body, but the body was incapable of pulling itself up. She was defeated. Defeated by Destiny.

It was Destiny, however, that helped her back up. Destiny Jones leaned down with a huge smile on her face and pulled Colette Samson back to her feet.

"I can't believe that didn't knock you out," Destiny said. "That punch should have knocked you the fuck out."

Colette didn't let on that she felt half-unconscious. Instead, she smiled at her friend and accepted the arm up. Destiny had a rock-hard body built from years of training. Her umber skin glistened with polished mahogany undertones shining through, a light layer of sweat giving her an otherworldly glow. Destiny's body wore spandex like a second layer of skin covering what could only be described as a heavenly body. Too busty to be a professional boxer, but too muscular to be a model. And yet, she was both. She was hated for her guts and beauty, envied by her friends, and never ignored.

Colette was one of the few women who were secure enough to have an actual friendship with Destiny. Colette didn't have time for jealousy, envy, or bitch cattiness. She was too busy driving herself to become the person she knew she could be. She never understood how people could waste their time and energy hating on someone who was using their talents and blessings instead of wasting them.

Spitting out her mouthguard, Colette shook her head. "It was a stupid rookie move. I lost control."

Destiny shook her head, laughing. "Yes, you did and yes it was. You blocked your vision with your own glove. There was no way I wasn't going to take that opening. It's not every day I get to throw a haymaker like that. Are you okay?"

Destiny's almond-colored eyes had big gold flecks in them, and the smile on her face showed some, but not too much concern.

Colette shoved Destiny away from her, playfully. "You wanna try that again, Bitch?"

Destiny laughed again. "Hey, come on, I was getting ready to go all Florence Nightingale on you. Keep your cool."

She put her arm around her friend's shoulders. "For a second, I thought I finally knocked you the fuck out. Damn girl, you sure can take a beating. Hey, wanna clean up and then go get a latte?"

Colette was laughing now too. The two women walked to the edge of the boxing ring and helped each other through the ropes. The other women in the gym moved back to their training with the match through. As Colette and Destiny made their way back to the locker room, the next training match moved into the ring. The sounds of jump ropes, weights, and work out bags created a comforting warmth that contrasted with the harsh cold world outside of the gym.

Unlike Destiny, Colette wasn't a model. She'd been offered jobs but had refused them all because her sights were set on a higher purpose. There's nothing wrong with modeling, but Colette had a particular obsession that drove her. It was an unhealthy obsession. Gold.

From the time she was a little girl she had been obsessed with the shiny metal. Some girls loved dolls or playing house, but Colette had played banker and goldsmith. She had collected pebbles and rocks and painted them gold, creating stacks in her closet. While her friends drew hearts and unicorns, she drew pirate chests, queens, and coins. She wasn't obsessed with it because of the monetary value. No, she wasn't one of those crass people who love money - no it was something about the metal itself. A warmth, a vibration, a texture. Colette loved gold.

She'd worked hard to acquire as much of it as she could. At 39, she was one of the most successful gold traders in the United States. Buying and selling shares wasn't her passion, but she was good at it. That morning she'd sold at a peak and then watched the price drop like an anchor. She repurchased the shares she had sold and was left with a $300,000 profit. This was money that she usually would have re-invested in additional shares but instead, something told her to keep it.

It was her 40th birthday.

Walking out of the gym, she was met with an unexpected billboard that had been put up across the street.

"Lordy, Lordy, Colette Forty!" The board screamed in ten-foot letters. Her face must have looked as shocked as she felt because Destiny immediately began laughing again. "Happy Birthday, Colette! You didn't think I'd forget, did you? I was going to get you a card, but I thought this was better. Do you like it?"

"I'm tempted to tell you to get back in that ring, but it's my birthday, and I don't really fancy another ass kicking, so let's go get some coffee." Neither woman was lacking in money. They were both at the top of their games.

"How much did that cost you?" Colette asked her. "It can't have been cheap."

"Oh, I didn't pay for it," Destiny said. "Actually, I got paid for it. Look—" She pointed to the rest of the billboard. On the billboard, a slightly blurred figure in silky lingerie was lowering herself into a spa's bath. Of course, it was Destiny. The bottom of the ad in smaller letters read 'Forty never felt so good! The New Youth Hamam Spa in Brooklyn."

"I suggested it to them months ago. They loved it. The hard part was getting them to agree to put this billboard up last night, but, you know," Destiny smiled, "I'm hard to say no to."

Colette was suddenly not so pleased "Wait a minute, me turning forty is their new slogan? I'm not so sure I like this a bit."

"Well, it's too late now," Destiny said "Happy Birthday, Bitch."

Collette would have to live with it. And besides, she wasn't going to let this ruin her day. Even if she'd never wanted to be famous. Destiny was a master puppeteer, and it wasn't just agencies that she made dance to her tune. Colette refused to be baited. It wasn't just the boxing ring Destiny was dangerous in.

"Let me get this straight, you just said to them 'Lordy, Lordy, Collette Forty!" and they went for it?"

Destiny flashed a big smile. "You know better than that. Nobody listens to models. It's not like they say 'Hey, let's hear what that beautiful gal with the perfect tits thinks of this?' Nope. I had to work my magic. Do you remember that guy Donnie Cohen from Holly Byoko's reception last year?"

Colette didn't, but it didn't matter.

Destiny went on. "He's a bigwig in the agency that runs this account, so I gave him a call and asked if he wanted to have lunch. He's married, but you know how those guys are, he couldn't say yes fast enough. So there we were, having lunch and he probably felt like he was getting somewhere. I mean I could feel his pulse rising. I mentioned the shoot I was supposed to do with New Youth Hamam Spa and how much I hated their slogan—it really was awful 'Scrub away your years'—like fucking ewww—anyway, at this point he was really looking for a way to make me happy so he rolled all over himself to agree with me even though he's probably the one who thought the stupid slogan up."

Colette loved this part of being Destiny's friend. Hearing how she worked her magical manipulation to make the world into exactly what she wanted. "Go on," she said.

"I could tell that he was making himself hate it more every moment, and he was desperate for something that would make me happy, so I picked up my phone and looked at it like I was getting a text message or looking at an appointment, and I said 'Lordy, Lordy, Colette Forty!' and girl, he took that hook fast. 'That's brilliant' he told me and of course I played coy 'What's that?' 'Lordy Lordy, Colette Forty—we can play on that, show that forty is the new youth. I love it, you're a genius Destiny.' and that's when I told him that it was his idea, not mine. After all, I was just commenting on something on my phone, it was his genius that realized it was a perfect slogan."

Colette laughed. "So'd you fuck him?"

Destiny looked at her with hurt in her eyes. "Hell no, I told you he was married. I might have led him on a little, but that's not my style. I just gave him the idea—and maybe later when I needed that billboard put up, I called him up and mentioned how I was thinking of joining a club his wife belongs to, but probably wouldn't if that particular billboard was used for the campaign."

"You really are an evil genius," Colette said. "Thank God you're on the side of the light."

"Oh, don't be too sure about that," Destiny said. "Light is a little too close to white for me to side with."

Colette not only made money trading gold, but she also had become one of the top jewelry designers in the world. Her gold jewelry used the metal in new ways that others hadn't thought of, but when people saw her jewelry, they always felt like they were looking at classical designs. Wispy ropes and delicate looking portraiture—all done in gold.

About a block before they reached the cafe, the two women passed a shop that neither had noticed before. It was called 'Thahab' and it looked like a typical high end handbag boutique, but there was something very different that caused both to stop. It took Colette a moment to recognize it.

"That fabric is woven with gold in it," she said to Destiny. "I've never seen anything quite like it. The threads are making patterns within the patterns of the textiles." The window display was a kaftan robe, a handbag, and a ring/bracelet combo that looked like a living thing as it crawled from the mannequin's finger and up its arm. "We're going in."

Destiny's arm had apparently turned to rubber because Colette didn't have to twist it at all. Inside the shop was a riot of Berber patterns and beautiful textures. Not every item had the gold weaving, but those that did stood out with a sort of magical shimmer. The shelves were sparsely populated with pottery, iron, and modern fashion that looked like it was ancient. The air was thick with the smell of spice and a light noise of crowds came from what must have been hidden speakers. Except for the lone clerk behind a standing desk, they were alone in the boutique.

"Is the jewelry in the window for sale?" Colette asked him.

"Oui, madame." He moved to the window display and removed the entire arm from the mannequin. It was a disturbing move. "C'est ca," he said, handing it to her. It was beautiful, and she wanted to handle it. The little Frenchman made no effort to help her remove it, he just watched as she struggled to hold the arm and remove the jewelry. Destiny moved in to help. As they worked a tiny white Pomeranian came running through the curtain at the back of the shop. It jumped up on Colette which annoyed her, but the dog was so small it didn't upset her balance in any way. Colette was more of a cat person.

Finally, getting the jewelry free of the arm, she handed the arm back to the clerk. He took the arm and moved to an ornately carved wooden chair in the corner where he leaned the arm against the wall and took a seat! He pulled a book from the shelf and began reading. Completely ignoring them. Destiny and Colette looked at each other in disbelief. The man's large head was fringed by a friar's wreath of cloud white hair, and when he sat she could see that he was wearing bright, multi-colored socks—like those of a circus clown. He was such an odd little man that she momentarily forgot about the jewelry she was holding as she looked at the little fool and felt an attitude of superiority radiate from his silence.

"I'm going to buy this for you," Destiny said. "I didn't actually think about the fact that I was telling the world you were turning forty. This is my apology."

"Excuse me," Destiny said to the man sitting in the corner, now with the dog in his lap. "How much is this?" Colette could hear the annoyance in Destiny's voice—no one ignored her—ever.

"Hello? We'd like to buy this." The man stood up, dropping the dog from his lap to the floor.

"Would you like the arm as well?" he asked her. It was one of the most bizarre questions Colette had ever heard. Even more bizarre was Destiny's answer.

"Yes, please wrap up the arm. What's the total?"

"$38,574 and ninety-nine cents," he said to her with no smile on his face.

Destiny took the jewelry from Colette's hand and threw it at him.

"Fuck you, man. Let's go." She grabbed Colette by the arm and began pulling her from the shop. The man set the jewelry on the counter and grabbed a business card. Moving faster than seemed possible, he pressed it into Colette's hand before Destiny had dragged her out the door.

Colette glanced at it before shoving it in her pocket.

Thahab - Exquisite Items
Pierre-Antoine DeFou – Proprietor

Destiny was livid with anger as they resumed their walk to the cafe. "Can you believe that shit?"

Colette had also been shocked by the price. The weight of it might have merited a price of $2000 and the craftsmanship and provenience might have taken it as high as $10,000, but she couldn't imagine what would have nearly quadrupled that price. She was shocked by the price but didn't understand Destiny's anger.

"That racist little motherfucker," she cursed. "I should go back and hit that stuck up French midget and kick his little dog." Colette wasn't sure it was racism, but she was white, and she knew enough about her privilege to know that her friend had a better sense of these things and that she wouldn't help anything by saying so.

"He heard me say I was going to buy it, and then he raised the price. That's some serious bullshit."

It was hard for Colette to stay quiet—she had to say something "And what was that shit with the arm?" she finally said. "Have you ever experienced anything like that?"

Destiny laughed now and looked at her friend. "Yeah, that was something else. Maybe he's just crazy and watching the shop for his brother or something. There was definitely something off about him. Did you see him just drop the dog on the floor?" Now she was laughing. "Maybe it wasn't racist—just some seriously maladjusted crazy person shit?"

"Did you see his socks?" Colette was glad Destiny was moving on.

Destiny laughed harder. "Hey, I'm sorry I didn't buy that for you, but that price was way out of line. I'll make it up to you."

"You already have," Colette said. It was no easy thing finding a best friend in this world. Destiny loved her for who she was. There was no better gift. "But I'm going to make you pay for those fucking billboards—someday."

Colette already knew she would be going back to the shop. She just wouldn't be taking Destiny with her when she went.

The Foolish Magician

Chapter 2: The Foolish Magician

Colette returned to Thahab the next day. She wasn't sure what she expected, but what she got was exactly the same treatment from exactly the same person. Monsieur DeFou didn't greet her as she walked in, didn't ask if she had returned for the bracelet/ring, and ignored her completely. Once again, he was sitting in the ornately carved chair with the dog on his lap.

"Excuse me," Colette said "I came to find out more about the jewelry I was looking at yesterday."

Monsieur DeFou looked up from his book. "I'm afraid it has been sold."

"What? Really?" She hadn't expected that. "Do you have anything like it?"

"No, Madame," he said to her. "There is nothing else like it."

"Well, who bought it?" She had to know what happened to it.

DeFou stood up, again dumping the dog from his lap onto the floor. "It's really best that you forget all about it," he told her. "It is gone and our policy is to protect the confidentiality of our patrons." He moved to the far wall and began moving a pile of vibrant but ancient textiles from one shelf to another.

A large ring of golden keys clattered out from between two of the pieces. It landed on the floor like a gymnast with a broken body, keys splayed in many directions. Colette gasped, seeing the keys cleared her mind of everything that had been in it before.

She had never seen anything like them. There were somewhere around twenty skeleton keys on the large golden ring. The ring itself was ornate and appeared to be decorated with rubies. The smallest of the keys was at least six inches and the largest was over a foot. Colette still hadn't done anything with the profits she had made before, and she still hadn't bought herself a birthday present.

The crazy little Frenchman leaned down and picked them up. "Ah, I'd wondered where these had gone. I wouldn't want to lose them." He put the ring on his wrist—it sparkled and glinted in the light. Without the keys, it would have looked like a priceless bangle by itself. With the keys, it was simply breathtaking.

"Ah, oui. That's better. Merci." She wasn't sure who he was talking to since there was no one else in the store, but she noticed that he was smiling now. "Tres, tres bien."

"Just out of curiosity," Colette asked him "How much are those keys?"

He looked at her with widened eyes, his white wispy hair appeared to poof out like a smoke ring as his albino caterpillar eyebrows shot upwards. "Ah Madame, I'm afraid I couldn't. They belong to my ancestral home, a palace built by my ancestors, a mysterious and powerful riad which contains forces too strong for this world. These keys to that riad are worth far more than their weight in gold. I assure you they are beyond your means."

"Oh, that's too bad," Colette said, uncharacteristically seeming to be giving up before she'd really begun. She would not play his game by his rules. "Where's your ancestral home? Nice? Paris? Grenoble?"

Pierre-Antoine began to laugh "Oh, no Madame. Originally, we came from Morocco. My family is Jewish, you see, and we left after the troubles began. All these years, I've been holding the deed, but none of us really want to go back. Those days are done and will never return."

"Why don't you sell it?" Colette asked.

"Why don't you make an offer," the little magician countered, catching her completely off guard. He smiled and began to turn away.

If the keys were more than the bracelet had been, then she could only imagine how much the home would cost.

Speaking in amusement to herself more than to DeFou, she said "I do have $300,000 I'd like to do something with."

"Oui, I accept your offer." She wanted to reach out and shake him, but of course, there was nothing binding in what had just happened. He looked at her and then turned away. "I'll have our family lawyers draw up the contract for you this evening. You can come and take care of the paperwork tomorrow. I suggest that you bring your attorney. I'll have the photos and deeds ready for you. I'm not sure why I've accepted an offer so low, but something tells me that it is meant to be. Au demain."

He turned and walked through the curtain in the back.---

"No way, Colette. No freaking way. I am not going to let you do this." Destiny was standing with her outside the bank. It was a cold day in the city and both women wore heavy black coats with gray wolf fur trim around the hoods.

Destiny had been arguing with Colette about her decision since the moment she had flippantly made an offer and Monsieur DeFou had accepted it without a moment's hesitation. There was no way that he should have accepted it. It was too little for too much or maybe the other way around. She was having a hard time seeing this deal clearly.

Destiny was sure it was some sort of a scam. Colette had considered that it might be, but after a week of due diligence, she was now pretty sure it wasn't. She didn't know what it was, but she didn't think she was being scammed. If anything, she felt like maybe she should offer him more, but that was just silly.

A house, an orchard, a vineyard, and that big ring of keys.

She still wasn't completely clear if she had made the offer or not. It wasn't like her to speak out loud, and there was a part of her that was convinced she had simply thought it. But, the proof was in the paperwork he had laid out for her and her attorney the next day.

Three-hundred thousand dollars. —not even enough to buy a small loft in New York City, but apparently, more than enough to buy a Jewish riad and the land around it in the town of Sanhaja, Morocco.

Colette was not a fool when it came to money, but Destiny was convinced she was making a terrible decision as the result of a female mid-life crisis. Colette had done her homework though. Monsieur Defou had been incredibly helpful and forthright when answering her questions. The house was nearly 300 years old, built by his 5th great grandfather, Conver DeFou. Conver had emigrated from France, wandered through the middle-Atlas mountains, and somehow met Sarah bin Ali S'rouda, a Berber Jewess living outside the walled city of Sefrou in a mini-citadel town called Sanhaja al-Casbah.

Having decided to stay, Conver moved his bride to a tiny farmhouse near a cascade and then began to build his masterpiece. Riad Conver was described by Pierre-Antoine as a sprawling wonderland of a house with doors that led nowhere, balconies with no doors, and hidden passages tucked behind walls and under floors. His memories were those of a small child in a large house and he possessed no pictures of the interior of house, but the deed he held was solid and the exterior was palatial.

Colette had hired a friend who specialized in international real estate to make sure that she understood the ins and outs of foreigners owning land in Morocco. She had further checked out the title and deed and informed Colette that both were clear, and the house and land were valued at considerably more than Colette was paying. When she found out the price, her friend offered to buy the house if Colette chose to back out. There was no backing out though. Colette was a force of nature that once set on a course was impossible to check—as Destiny was finding out.

"Destiny, you're not going to talk me out of this. My mind is completely resolved. I— Pierre Antoine now joined them. He was now a completely changed man. Gone was the funny little fool in brightly colored socks and in his place was a serious man in a dark suit with a beautiful wooden briefcase. There was something magical about the transformation, and as he came closer to the two ladies, Pierre-Antoine swept off his hat and made what would have been a comical little bow had he made it when last they had met, but now, was both charming and full of grace.

With a twinkle in his eye, Monsieur DeFou said "Doing business—with both of you—has been and continues to be an immense pleasure. Shall we go inside and finalize things?" Destiny looked ready to explode but seemingly contained herself. DeFou smiled at her as he held the door. There was no real reason for Destiny to be there, she had simply wanted to dissuade Colette from making a very expensive mistake.

Looking at them both, she shook her head. "I don't think I'm going to be able to stop either of you so there's no need for me to be here. Colette, I hope you don't regret this." She turned and stalked off into the cold morning.

With Destiny gone, there was no more resistance to the deal. Colette's birthday present was about to be finalized.

Stepping into the bank, the two were met at reception and were led to the bank manager's office where the paperwork had been prepared. It was a glass cubicle open to the rest of the bank. The curtains had been drawn open. Colette's agent had gone the extra mile to make sure that everything was on the up and up— even to the point of getting Colette's bank manager to take a hand in the paperwork and documentation. The receptionist asked them to wait for the manager and left them.

Monsieur DeFou sat on the black leather sofa and fiddled with his briefcase a bit. Suddenly, he was a funny little man pretending to be a serious little man. He set the briefcase on the glass coffee table and turned to Colette. "Would you like to see something interesting?" he asked.

She smiled awkwardly at him but finally nodded assent and said "Sure, that would be nice."

He opened his wooden briefcase. It was like that moment where the boss opens the magic package in *Pulp Fiction*—she had her eyes on the box and wouldn't have been surprised to see an otherworldly light suddenly erupt from it. That wasn't what happened though.

Instead, Monsieur DeFou pulled out a tiny blue glass bottle and a set of tiny blue cups both decorated with gold filigree work. He set them on the magazine table in front of them and then pulled out a small tree branch and a curved silver knife. All had been set into the case with elastic bands that held them inside. Next, he revealed a small red velvet bag which he loosened and poured into his open hand.

"These are silver coins made about 50 years before the birth of Christ. The woman on them is often said to be the goddess Isis, but really, she is Cleopatra, the Queen. I have twenty-three of them." He handed one to her. "On the other side is an eagle riding a lightning bolt. It's strikingly similar to the eagle used by the United States on the great seal. Don't you think?"

Colette wasn't sure why he had brought the odd assortment of things with him but was keenly aware of the fact that she had never held anything so ancient. He had a way of compelling your attention that was all but impossible to ignore. The woman on the face of the coin was beautifully rendered, and the coin itself looked like it might be just a few years old, not a few thousand.

"They're beautiful," she told him. "But why did you bring these things?"

"Miss Samson," he said looking up at her, once again masterful "I am a silly old man. These are the things of tradition. Among my people, we have certain days and rituals that we perform. I don't know if we believe in them any longer or not, but the important thing is that tradition is upheld. For example, before we conduct business—it is very important that we share a bit of honey-lemon water. Why? I don't know. But I will be very pleased if you will join me for this traditional drink."

He motioned to the blue bottle. Colette knew she should be wary, but instead she was charmed once again and quickly agreed. At this point it was counterproductive to argue. She wanted the keys and all that went with them more than she had ever wanted anything. Monsieur DeFou lined up two cups and opened the bottle. It made a loud hiss as he opened it. He poured the water into the cups and from somewhere a lemon appeared in his hand. He turned to Colette, "Would you be so kind as to cut the lemon?"

"There isn't anywhere to cut it—" she began to protest but Pierre-Antoine was already handing her the strange knife. She pulled the blade from its metal sheath. It was a beautiful piece of workmanship. Setting the coin down in Pierre-Antoine's case, she picked up the lemon and began to gingerly cut it. The fact that she was cutting lemon for a drink in the lobby of her bank before spending a fortune on a property she had never seen seemed irrelevant, only the act of cutting the lemon seemed important now. The other people in the bank—the customers, the clerks— all seemed to ignore them. It was as if an invisible barrier hid them from the outside world.

The room had taken on a strange glow and things were now moving much slower than reality normally did. As Colette cut the lemon in two, Monsieur DeFou's hand suddenly darted out like a snake from amongst a basket of apples.

"Be careful," he hissed, grabbing Colette's hand and pulling it back from where she had seemingly been about to impale it on the blade she was wielding. A small spot of blood appeared on the center of her palm. The two halves of the lemon had fallen into the wooden briefcase below.

"Mademoiselle, a slip like that can easily cause a pain that won't disappear for months." She had no idea how the knife had moved so fast.

He reached down to pick up the lemon. Colette noticed a small spot of blood on the rim of one of the lemon halves. It was that one which Pierre-Antoine squeezed into the cups. He gingerly took the blade back and fitted it back into the sheath.

"To your health and property," he offered one of the cups to her and lifted the other for himself.

"And to yours," Colette said. The words felt uncomfortably formal as she said them.

As the liquid passed her lips she felt a fiery warmth begin above her head. The heat passed into her head and began coursing through her body until it ran out of her feet. Spider webs and the spiders in them hidden in the tall dark corners of the bank manager's office zoomed into her consciousness. She had never felt more present or alive. At that moment...

The door opened. The bank manager came barreling into the room. "Sorry for the delay folks, but I think we've got everything done properly now. I'll just need your signatures, and then we'll notarize the forms. The money will be transferred immediately, and everything will be hunky-dory." He didn't seem to notice the case, the glasses, the bottle, or the strange feeling that filled the room. While he spoke, Monsieur DeFou put everything away.

They each signed the appropriate documents which transferred the title to Colette and the money to DeFou. In just a few minutes, the entire process was complete. The bank manager left again after shaking their hands and wishing them a nice day. The spiders up in their corners had barely had time to stir. Colette's awareness of them faded, and she was no longer so acutely aware of them.

As they stood to leave, one of the coins dropped from Pierre-Antoine's briefcase, probably the one Colette had been holding. He reached down and picked it up, looked at it, and then handed it to her.

"I still have twenty-two, but it seems that this queen of the coins wants to come with you. It would be my pleasure if you would accept it as a small token of my esteem."

Colette felt like the coin already belonged to her, which was a mysterious truth.

It wasn't until that evening that it occurred to Colette that she had everything, but the thing that had gotten her into all of this. Pierre-Antoine had not brought the keys with him. How in the world had she missed that? It seemed she had been so occupied by the ritual of the blue glass bottle, the ancient coins, and the sliced lemon—not to mention the signing of the deeds—that she had forgotten all about her big, beautiful ring of keys. She would go get them in the morning.

The Egyptian Priestess

Chapter 3: The Egyptian Priestess

That night she slept restlessly as a growing anxiety tickled her brain. She was terrified that it had all been a con-job. Even though she had the deed and title, all of the paperwork had been legitimized, and her hired expert had assured her that she was getting a great deal. She tossed and turned through the night creating scenario after scenario in which she had been had. By morning, it had built to a fever pitch. Even as she rushed down Fifth Avenue, a feverish voice in her brain said "You're not getting those keys—"

Colette recognized that she was feeling an unhealthy fixation on the keys themselves. It was those keys that had gotten her into this mess, somehow mesmerizing her and getting her to buy a property she had never seen. Yes, she already owned it—but somehow that didn't matter if she didn't have the keys.

What if the keys were gone?

She felt her panic swell to a crescendo, and by an act of sheer will she suppressed a reactive wave of anger. She would find Pierre-Antoine and take the keys from him. Her anger screamed "I will make him pay!"

"And besides," she told herself "It is the property that really matters."

But she knew she was lying. It was the property and the riad which were the symbol and the keys that were of the utmost importance. It was the keys she had been after all along. The rest was just something that came with the keys.

The windows of the shop were painted over with a liquidation sign. The shop wasn't closed, but in an instant all of her fears were regrouping into a tight ball of anxiety that instantly grew to fill all the space within her skin. She grasped the door, pushed it open. and stepped into a maelstrom of chaotic energy.

All of this madness filled her the instant she opened the door. On the heels of it, the logical part of her mind reminded her that she owned the riad, she owned the property, and she owned the keys. They were hers, and she would get them. Nothing would stop her. They were just a symbol for something else in her psyche, something she felt she needed. Even if they were lost, she could replace them. The keys were unimportant or at the very least, not as important as she was making them out to be.

"How odd I've suddenly become," she thought to herself as she pushed the door closed behind herself. She had become obsessive about something as curious and unimportant as an old set of keys. Yes, they were beautiful, but her obsession with them had caught her by surprise even at the same moment that she had recognized that obsession. She paused, looking at her reflection in the mirror on the wall of Thahab.

Her blue-eyed reflection looked back at her actual self with a tilted head, high cheekbones, and perfectly styled golden-brown hair. Her long perfectly shaped legs emerged from under her red London Fog raincoat. Ankles sculpted as if by Cellini—which were always the answer to silly party questions about her favorite body part. Given her goddess-like measurements, people always thought she was being demure or funny when she claimed her ankles as divine, but in truth, there was no other part of her physical self that brought her such joy.

Several deep breaths and a forced smile to hide anxiety. Such was her stress level that she hadn't even seen the state of Thahab despite standing in it. As she established control, her tension began to dissipate, and she stepped forward with fears vanquished, her logical mind once again in charge. This obsessiveness, now clinically observed, told her that something had shifted within her and was trying to find a place to settle. Her perfectly ordered inner world was in chaos. Lordy, Lordy, Colette Forty.

Handbags and packing materials were scattered pell-mell as sophisticated looking women went through them like impoverished spinsters at a rummage sale. She quickly surveyed the shop but didn't find a man in it. Pierre-Antione, his chair, and his dog were nowhere to be seen. A regal woman with dark hair and an Egyptian temple style dress stood behind the counter watching the proceedings and shouting answers to women who lifted brightly colored handbags demanding prices.

"$650"

"$425"

"That one is half-price but still $1200."

She smiled at Colette between pricings. Colette swallowed the scream she felt inside her "Where are my keys?" —it was an act of will more powerful than ignoring the desire to wipe away rivulets of sweat in the boxing ring, but she overcame the desire. She smiled back at the woman as she wove her way between frantic uptown shoppers. Colette controlled her raging anxiety and refrained from shrieking, "Out of my way, you bag toting bitches!"

"Ladies! We're going to be closing in five minutes. Please bring your purchases to the counter and I'll ring you up—if you aren't in the queue in the next minute or two, you will have to come back later today when we re-open at 4 pm." The woman's voice was deep and throaty from a lifetime of Pall-Malls. She had a jazz singer's rasp on a deeply resonant voice of authority. Her tone was feminine and melodic, but had just the right amount of sandpaper to make it sexy. Her temple gown accentuated that observation. Not many women could pull that outfit off. She was in her mid-forties, possibly even her fifties and wore heavy gold armbands around her biceps and a golden collar that perfectly accentuated her olive skin. The light blue temple dress and 1920's bob haircut completed her look. A purple sash demurely and elegantly covered her shoulders.

Colette stood in the doorway, demanding her attention, but the chaos had moved from the stacks on the floor to the growing queue, and she had no choice but to fall into the line if she wanted to be seen. She was last, but she had a place, and she would be seen. Her restless nervousness grew until she thought she might explode. She imagined lashing out at the women around her with fists of furious anxiety while screaming about the relative unimportance they and their handbags held in comparison with her missing keys. In that ridiculous fantasy, she regained her composure and calmed herself.

The cashier's dark eyes looked up from time to time and surveyed the women and their purchases. The deep black mascara and blue eyeshadow contributed to her powerful mystique even as she rang shoppers up. Her eyes lingered on Colette, taking in the fact that she held nothing to purchase.

Fire hydrant red lipstick and long black eyelashes drew attention from the immense amount of gold ornament she wore, something which Colette immediately noticed. As a jewelry designer, Colette was acutely aware of jewelry—especially gold— and she immediately decided that the woman was wearing actual gold jewelry—not costume or gold-plate. This 'clerk' was wearing someone's annual income in jewelry. There was more to her than an aging shop girl.

Finally reaching the counter, Colette steeled herself to make the demand for her keys.

Before she could say a word, the woman looked up and said "You are she."

"Excuse me?"

"The woman who bought the keys, that is you, correct?" Somehow it sounded natural that this woman would say she had bought the keys and not the house. It was how she had been thinking of it all morning. It was the source of her panic.

"That's right, but Monsieur DeFou forgot to give them to me at the bank…---"

"Oh no, he didn't forget. My brother never forgets anything." Colette was surprised by that, this woman looked far too young to be the sister of the shop proprietor.

"You're brother? How is that possible? He's at least…---" Colette realized she was about to guess the woman's age out loud, a serious faux-pas she refused to make. "He seems far older than you."

The woman laughed. "Oh, you are kind, but we are both far older than we look. I have simply taken better care of myself and as a result he's aged much worse than I have. My makeup and jewelry certainly help to hide my years."

"Yes, I suppose it does. Your jewelry is magnificent." Despite herself, Colette was drawn into the woman's story while, for the moment, forgetting the entire purpose of her being there. The speech she had prepared while waiting in line was as invisible as the lines of age that were missing from the woman's face. She stood transfixed as the woman came around the counter and moved towards the door. She pulled the blinds and locked them both inside before turning with a smile.

"Like I said, he didn't forget. I asked him to distract you so that I could give them to you. I told him that I wanted to meet you and this seemed like the best way."

Colette remembered the keys, remembered her reason for coming to the shop. "But what about my—the keys? When will I get them?"

"I have them here." The woman reached under the counter and brought the keys up in her perfectly shaped hand. As she handed the ring of keys to Colette, a sudden weight was lifted from her soul. An electric wind ran through the room, and the woman smiled and held out her hand in greeting.

"My name is Chloestibel, but my friends call me Chloe. I do hope that you will forgive me for this subterfuge, but I wanted to share some important details about that which you have purchased. Not least among them being why you've done so. I felt it was very important that we have a chance to sit down together."

Colette took her hand and introduced herself. "Well, you already know that I am Colette, but still it is nice to meet you Chloe—although I wonder if this meeting might have been easier if we had simply done it another way."

Chloe didn't let go of her hand and instead led her to a wooden bench off to the side of the room.

"Where is your brother? Why has he closed the shop?" Colette had so many questions and wasn't absolutely positive where to begin with them. That seemed a good place.

"I don't have these answers, Colette. He is like that, he sets out on his own from time to time leaving the rest of us to clean up whatever might have occupied him. A few months or years later, he pops up somewhere, and we all gravitate to wherever he might be. We are an odd family, but very close. Our rituals and lifestyle usually don't make sense to those around us. Did he do the thing with the blue bottle?"

Colette was startled by the question. "Yes, he explained about the tradition, but I cut my hand by accident—"

Chloe laughed, a cynical throaty laugh. "That was no accident, that is how it always happens— Listen, I want to share a few family secrets with you—things that Pierre-Antoine might not have told you. By taking ownership of this house, you have by proxy become a part of our extended family. Don't worry, we won't be dropping by to borrow money, it's not that kind of family, but some knowledge could be important for you."

Colette felt uncomfortable being brought into this odd family's business, but then, she had bought their ancestral home, so she nodded and waited for Chloe to continue.

"The house and property that you've bought was built with a specific philosophy in mind. Like most houses it has four walls forming the base of the structure. In this case, the walls are aligned with the points of a compass. Each point of the house is a cardinal direction. So, for example, the front door is in a wall with a corner that is North and a corner that is East. Walk out the door and you are facing Northeast."

"In life, it is our family's long held belief that symbols often help us to understand the world. For example, east. East is the direction for family, home, the feminine and the things of the earth. Gold for example is an eastern element. As women who love jewelry—we are very oriented towards the east."

"North, on the other hand, is the element of the mind and thought. It is the element of conflict and reason, and when combined with east, it indicates a battle that must be fought to establish a home. The door was put in the north-east wall for a reason. I've pointed you in the right direction, but you will have to find the true reason on your own. I can only tell you so much, but the action is up to you."

Colette listened while she fidgeted lovingly with the ring of keys—"These keys,." she said. "What is it about them? Why do they feel so—important?"

Chloe peered into her face, for the moment, looking ancient. "Inside the riad there are ten doors. Outside of the riad there is one door. Under the riad there are many more doors. These are the keys to all the locks that open those doors."

Colette nodded. "You mentioned the north and east corners. What about south and west?"

Chloe smiled in approval. "South is the direction of the wind. Spring, air, warmth, fire. South is the direction of the spiritual, and it is this direction one should go when looking for answers. West, west is the direction of love, the heart and emotions."

"The riad, it is built with these four cardinal points and their influence in mind. What you find inside will be more easily understandable if you are able to orient yourself to the proper direction and look at things from this perspective. Like life, everything can be explained by these four concepts."

Colette was mesmerized by this suddenly very spiritual encounter with what she now recognized as an ancient soul.

"The combinations of the material world, the mental world, the spiritual world, and the emotional world are the colors that paint the canvas of our reality. There is no situation which cannot be accurately explained using a combination of the four directions. Our present world is ruled by the materialist perspective. The scientific revolution emphasized the mental perspective."

"Not so long ago in the Victorian era, there was a far more heavy romantic influence and further back, the spiritual held sway. Each element, each direction, each time has a period of influence and conflict. The northern winds are currently carrying us, but eventually, that too must change."

"The world can be explained by all of this. It's important for you to know this before you go to the riad."

Colette honestly asked the simplest and most important of questions "Why?"

Chloe smiled with centuries of wisdom and worlds of compassion. "That is the question you need to constantly be asking, child, because it is the only way to discover the answer. I'm afraid there's nothing more I can tell you. I hope this is enough."

The Empress

Chapter 4: The Empress

Colette's travel arrangements should have been simple, but they quickly became far too complex. Her plan was to do a sort of *Eat, Pray, Love* trip. She loved the book and hated the movie. She wasn't trying to find herself through traveling and having adventurous affairs, but she planned to use her time to get to know herself better, and a foreign culture meant that she would be able to do that without the distractions of home.

Her initial plan was to fly from New York to Paris. From Paris she would fly to Morocco, and then after visiting the riad in Morocco she would go to Barcelona, take a few days for an island retreat on Tenerife in the Canary Islands and then finally, back to Barcelona, back to Paris, and back to New York. She'd planned it as a six-week holiday/adventure.

The first problem arose in Paris. A bag-handler strike had closed virtually every flight from Paris to Morocco, so once she arrived in Paris, she learned that the only flights to Morocco in France were from Marseille. From Marseille, she could catch a flight to Casablanca. She would have to take a train to Marseille which meant a few days extra in France, but that was not such a problem. The problem was really something else entirely.

The problem was 'the Empress'. It was the sarcastic nickname she had been calling her mother since her teenage years.

The Empress, The Queen of Everything, Her Ladyship—they all carried the same meaning and honestly, her mother wouldn't have batted an eyelid at hearing them—in fact, she was likely to approve of it!

Susan Hemmings-Samson was one of those waspy New York socialites who insist upon keeping a remnant of familial royal heritage close enough that it was certain to fall within noticing range of everyone around her. Her grandfather had been the brother of the Earl or Duke or Baron of something or other, or perhaps it was her grand-uncle—the exact relationship was never made clear to Colette, but often referred to by the and *pretensified* form of '*my dear uncle the Duke*' during polite conversation. Susan wasn't so gauche as to say "We come from royalty" but her every movement and action told whomever she was talking with that it was so. Most importantly, she was just the type of woman who could pull it off without anyone making fun of her. No one dared question her vague royal lineage—except her daughter.

When her mother found out that Colette was taking a trip and had bought a 'palace', she insisted on making her daughter's departure a social event—even though Colette asked her not to. She invited her snooty socialite friends for an afternoon of crumpets and tea. She insisted that Colette attend, and though it was the day before her departure—Colette found herself unable to say no.

"Darling, you *muuust* come. What will Mrs. Brixton think if you leave without saying goodbye?" Colette wasn't quite sure who Mrs. Brixton was or why what she thought mattered, but she did owe it to her mother and her friends to give them something to talk about—it was these women who had given her the initial start in the jewelry design business. Many of them were among her top clients. Some of them had obscene amounts of money to spend, while others simply had to keep up the appearance of a legitimate family reputation amidst declining family fortunes.

Colette's mother wore an ostentatious white dress and was sitting on the verandah of her garden when Colette arrived. It was Colette's insistence on an afternoon tea garden party that had kept this from becoming a true 'social event'. Her mother was peeling the skin from a pomegranate, seemingly oblivious to the danger this put her white dress in. That was her mother—Colette had no doubt that through the whole process not a single drop of blood red juice would be spilled on the fresh whiteness of that dress. Susan had flowing blonde hair which could have been the proud possession of a woman thirty years her junior. Her figure matched. It was only her face that showed the passage of time. Her skin had wrinkled like a bleached raison left too long in the sun.

The tea party was a gathering of aged women in dresses too fancy for daily wear and funny hats. They took delicate sips of expensive tea with their pinkies extended nearly as far as their privilege. A delicious assortment of sandwiches, crusts removed, fed a collection of women who had once been the darlings of the socialite scene. Over time, of course, many had their teeth removed, and the majority of them had also been removed from the top tiers of society due to their 'eccentricities', loss of family fortune, or fading influence. Her mother reigned supreme over this court of oft forgotten and twice removed aristocracy.

"Darling," her mother motioned her over. She wore a small diamond tiara which sparkled in the light and created a magical aura of her hair and those bright blue eyes shining from her tiny wrinkled face. She made small motioning gestures with her free hand—the other still holding the pomegranate, the seeds of which seemed to be lining themselves up in an orderly fashion on the plate beneath it. "Tell Mrs. Granita-Hollingsworth about your palace."

Colette sighed. She hadn't expected it, but she should have. Her mother, upon hearing that a riad was a sort of Moroccan palace, had immediately begun calling it a palace. When Colette explained that it was a glorified farmhouse and had been the family home of Jewish refugees, her mother had tut-tutted her. "A likely story, more likely the retreat of a dauphin or some displaced royal personage who needed to escape the intrigues of the Sun King's court."

The Empress had never let her imagination grow old. Like all women of her class, race, and age—she was raised with a casual institutional racism that she would deny, but she had immediately thrown the word Jewish out and instead began to refer to the riad as the palace of a French dissident.

"Colette, did you bring the keys?" She had not brought them, but that was no impediment to her mother who began to regale Mrs. Granita-Hollingsworth with stories of how the palace steward must have been a massive man to carry such a heavy weight of keys at his belt. "He was most certainly one of those giants from the Atlas Mountains, captured by the Prince and then trained as a personal valet—" Colette had never heard of giants in the Atlas Mountains, but then neither had her mother, Mrs. Granita-Hollingsworth, or the other ladies. They would all repeat the story over time and thus give it more reality, making the imaginary into the real—as happened frequently. It was one of the skills that made the Empress the social leader of her pack. Colette's mother could have been at home among the true elites, but as just one of many—not as the alpha female. She preferred to hold court over a collection that looked up to her, rather than making herself common. Better to be the queen of the beggars than a subject of another. She kept her admirers and sycophants like pets, and this was what raised her to the status she enjoyed.

"Colette." Her mother's eyes met hers with an intensity she had rarely seen before. "I must speak to you in private" To the gathered ladies she announced, "Pardon us, please. It's time for me to pass on some motherly advice before my girl goes running off on her adventures."

She said it as if she weren't talking about a successful, career minded woman who had just turned forty. Colette had no choice but to be led off by the elbow to her mother's sitting room.

"Darling. There is something you must know." Colette looked at her mother and waited. Her mother adored the dramatic and insisted that everyone play their role in the dramas she created around herself. "Now that you have reached forty, there is wisdom that I can share with you."

"Time is your greatest ally. If you can think further ahead than those around you, you can mold people's thinking to whatever it is you want them to think. It doesn't matter if you are working with rich or poor people, you need to be ahead of them in time. For time is the greatest of illusions, and only those with true insight recognize that the distant future is as close as the present. Like my beautiful garden, each section must be planned, the soil prepared, and the seeds laid at the proper time. Cultivating social status, relationships, and even repairing an old house—they all require this understanding of time. The present moment determines the future, and you can shape it to your own desire. I knew that this would be what my old age would be like when I was just a girl. I worked backwards from it to discover what I had to do to get here. The first steps seemed ridiculous to those around me. I dug up the Duke and brought him back to life. I made him more important in the future than he had ever been in the past or present. As long as my life exceeded his, I knew this was where I would be. You, my darling, you will do fine, but don't get in a rush and forget that the future is more about right now than the past is."

Colette had never heard her mother speak this way, with no pretense and no agenda. The smile-lines crinkling around her ancient blue eyes verified that the words had been long thought out and prepared in advance, just for her. She wasn't sure why her mother had chosen this moment to give her these words, but she carefully noted them and etched them into her consciousness.

And then the cunning pretense had returned "Now—I believe that Mrs. Crupfield-Jacobs has some questions she wants to ask about this Moroccan Prince you've inherited the palace from."

Good to Be King

Chapter 5: Good To Be King

Colette wasn't a fatalist, but a part of her had expected more problems than she encountered on the trip to Morocco. Yet—nothing unpleasant happened—in fact, it was almost boring. She had expected to run into problems with tickets, passports, border control, transfers—but even in Marseille where she had to catch a budget flight—everything went well. The only real drama of the entire trip was when some idiot had left his bag unattended in a boarding area—the result of which was some seriously melodramatic action with a bomb squad and a squad of uniformed police surrounding the suitcase—only to have the clown who left it come out of the bathroom and apologize.

Aside from that, it was a silky-smooth trip.

Arriving in Casablanca, she expected to find herself on a dusty airfield in some glorious recreation of a Humphrey Bogart movie where she was cast as Loren Bacall, but instead she emerged from her plane down a ramp. Mohammed V International Airport was a modern steel and glass terminal building complete with luxury shops. She could easily have been arriving in Boston rather than what she had always thought of as the most romantic city in Africa.

Still, an overwhelming sense of things being different slapped her in the face as she debarked the plane. Things were very different, but she couldn't put her finger on exactly how. Certainly, the architecture looked the same—at least inside the modern terminal. Still, it was different. The exact difference tickled the edges of her consciousness. Finally, she was able to corner the disorienting sense. It was the smell.

Cumin and cinnamon permeated the air in Morocco. Even within the terminal of the Mohammed V Airport Terminal. Morocco smelled different to anywhere else on Earth—that she had been. There was no denying it (and no reason to). She had an even harder time deciding whether or not she liked it.

The severe looking agents at customs worked methodically, and she could already see that her usual free form approach was going to be one of the big challenges in adjusting to Morocco. She would soon learn that in Morocco; to get anything done, one must have a plan. This was true on a large scale, but also apparent in the haphazard way people took to getting in line or in any of the things a person coming from the orderly west might take for granted. She could see that if she stood in the disorderly funnel shaped line passively—the flow of other travelers would simply keep her from moving. Standing in line was an active experience that required one to fight for their position.

'Expectation leads to disappointment,' this had been the wise counsel of the Buddha centuries before. She took that to heart as she arrived in Morocco because she could already see that whatever expectations she might have about this country—and about her riad—would need to be severely checked once she departed from the arrival area.

Colette was notoriously brave among those who knew her. Many of her friends would have described her as intrepid—this however—was not all that true. She had flown from the USA on a first-class flight and was the kind of traveler who enjoyed niche specialty tours, the kind that impressed her friends with being so different, but which were, after all, simply organized tours. She was not generally that breed of ultra-independent-superwoman-solo traveler they made her out to be. What she was, though, was open to adjusting her experience to fit with whatever the conditions on the ground might be. She was flexible, not intrepid. Looking at Morocco for the first time, she felt confident that she would need every bit of that flexibility.

Having decided that, it was a nice surprise when she was met at the arrival area by Simo, a heavy-set young Moroccan man with hints of a beard framing a jolly round face. The sign he held said "Madame Colette Samson. He had drawn a smiley face on it—something that she would have thought was forbidden in an Islamic country. It was the first of many times when her expectations about what Islamic would mean were completely and totally wrong. She'd hired Simo through an agency that specialized in helping foreigners find local assistants to assist them in navigating their way through Morocco. He was part driver, part guide, and part secretary.

She'd hired Simo to pick her up, act as her translator, and be her 'Man Friday' while she tried to figure out what she had gotten herself into. She'd looked for someone from Sanhaja, but there was no one she could find. She had contacted Simo's agency because they specialized in personal assistants for foreigners. Most of them spoke French instead of English. Simo, however, seemed to fit the bill of what she was looking for. He had a car, he spoke near fluent English, he was college educated, and he had a background in building and construction management. Seeing his big round smiling face atop the gray striped Djellaba he wore, she was certain she'd gotten lucky. His salary was $92 per day and that included the use of his car and gasoline. For her, it was a bargain, for Simo it was a fortune. The smiley face on the sign, and the smiley face on Simo both assured her that she had been blessed with the right person.

Culture shock is like a kidnapper. You might be walking along, feeling completely at ease in your surroundings, when suddenly, it hits you out of nowhere and throws a bag over your head, overwhelming your senses all at once. Colette was now the unwitting victim of that as she suddenly became aware of just how different this place was to everything she had ever known.

"Salam a lyceum," she said "You are Simo?"

"Wa leycum Salam. Oui, I am Simo. Welcome in Morocco Madame Samson. Marhabbakum." Hmmm...maybe his English wasn't as good as it was represented online, but it was good enough. He gave a funny little bow which reminded her of the odd old Monsieur DeFou. Really, Simo with his chubby belly and general roundness was nothing like the old magician, but there was an unmistakable something that connected the two. DeFou had been sharp where Simo was blunted. DeFou had been quite old (even older than she'd first suspected), but Simo was barely out of boyhood and still had the rounded body of a child wrapped around and over his dark features. He made her think of a puppy with his big dark eyes.

"You had a nice flight? Everything is okay for you?" He continued "Yes, I am Simo, and I am here to serve you and take care of all your many questions or consequences you may have."

Colette smiled at him. She was certainly glad to have someone who would take care of the consequences, though it was an ominous mis-statement. Hopefully, there would be no consequences.

As a child, her mother had often threatened her, "If you keep acting this way, you will have to live with the consequences!" She had thought 'The Consequences' were friends of her mother's, just like the Cunninghams and the Brightons were. Her mother was unaware of the misunderstanding until one day when five-year-old Colette burst out "But I don't want to live with the consequences, I want to live with you!"

Colette couldn't help it, a giggle escaped her at the memory and the idea that she might *have* 'The Consequences' at last. Thankfully she had Simo to take care of them.

Thinking of her mother, she realized that she didn't want to be treated like a royal. "Simo, please call me Colette. Madam Samson is my mother. Thank you for being here on-time."

Simo smiled with boyish charm and delight. "I've been here for seven hours Miss Colette; I thought it was best to sleep in the airport just in case you decided to come early." He took parts of her suggestion, but it was too informal, so he added the Miss to it. She decided to let it go. She kind of liked the sound of Miss Colette. It was far better than Miss Samson.

"Are all Moroccans as dedicated to their work as you?" She asked him.

Simo laughed. "No, they think me a bit odd, I'm afraid." Now there was a hint of British accent to his English, and Colette was certain his teachers had not been American. The accent was funny because it had some of the singsong of a Hindu with the richness of the African or Caribbean. In a word, Simo's accent was 'unique'.

Simo directed her attention to a nearby cafe in the concourse. "Most of the Moroccans, we sit in cafes all day and just wait for work to come to us. At least we pretend to be waiting for work and then at the end of the day go back home and tell her we looked the whole day long for a job."

"Who?" Colette asked. "Who do you tell? The woman of the house? You mean they tell their wives?"

Simo shook his head in the negative. "No, not usually. Their mums. The guys who sit in cafes don't marry unless they meet an older foreigner lady or if they get a poor girl in trouble. No one wants to marry their daughter to a bum."

Colette looked at the guys sitting in the cafe. Most of them looked older than her, some of them were old enough to be her father. "You mean those guys still live with their parents?"

Simo nodded. "Of course, if they haven't married, why in the world would they want to live anywhere else? Is this your only baggage?" He said it as if she were traveling light.

Her massive case weighed nearly a hundred pounds. Simo happily took the handle and pulled it behind him indicating that she should come along. "Let's get out of here. It's going to take us most of the day to get us to Sanhaja."

He began to walk. "Simo?" His smiling good nature had driven away the culture shock. The bag had been removed from her head. She felt immensely grateful.

He turned and looked at her, "Yes, Miss Colette."

She pointed to a picture on a billboard over the concourse. The man in the picture looked like an older version of Simo— remarkably so. He wore the same gray and black striped Djellaba, had the same peach fuzz on his jowls, and even had the same boyish rosy glow despite being decades older. The picture hung above the doors Simo had been about to lead her through. Doors which led directly outside and into the blazing African sun.

"Who is that man? Are you related to him?"

Simo looked pleased at her question, but he laughed mirthfully. He smiled and looked like he might laugh more but managed to hold it somewhere inside his jolly frame. He looked at her with joyous astonishment and said, "You must be joking Miss Colette. You don't know who he is?"

She had no idea. Given the placement and size of the image, she figured that he must be a famous star or entertainer. Simo's complex blend of delight and bafflement at her lack of knowledge and association between himself and the man in the picture told her that he was someone that she should definitely become familiar with.

"No, I'm sorry. Who is he?"

"Miss Colette, you must never forget his face and always be able to recognize him. That is the greatest man in the world. That is His Majesty Mohammad the Sixth, King of Morocco, descendant of the Prophet, and leader of the Faithful." There was an electric power in the air as Simo looked at the picture with the utmost devotion. She could have almost sworn that the lazy guys in the airport cafe sat up straighter in pride at that moment. They looked as if they might even go out and find a job, but then the moment had passed, and Simo was back again. "Do you really think I look like him?"

Colette found it hard to believe that she was the first to have ever mentioned the resemblance to Simo. It was so striking that she was almost certain it was purposely cultivated by the young man. Either way, she suddenly knew one thing for certain.

The King of Morocco was the biggest star in the country.

Authority Lessons

Chapter 6: Authority Lessons

Stepping out the glass doors of the Mohammed V Airport and into the dry heat of Morocco, Colette was hit again by the smell of the place. This time mixed in with the spices and coffee there was something else, the smell of burning plastic. Not as pleasant as her first impression, but she was happy to hold onto the first impression. You never get a chance to make a second first impression.

Moving across the drop off zone past taxis, crazily parked cars, and well-dressed Moroccan businessmen driving Renault and Citroens, Simo led her to a tan Mercedes diesel. The car looked like a tank from some Cold War era movie. Made from big blocky pieces of steel, it looked like it was a model from the 1980's, but Simo was obviously as meticulous about keeping his car in good condition as he was about being on time. It looked pristine.

He stowed her bags in the trunk and then moved to open the back door for her.

"Simo, I'd rather ride in the front." Colette had always been very egalitarian in this way and was rarely one to put herself visibly over someone else.

"Yes, Miss Colette. Of course, please get in the back of the car." The young man seemed distressed, and Colette was certain that she had finally reached a point where the language barrier was making things difficult.

"I don't like to ride in the back, Simo." There, he should understand that.

Simo left the back door open and pulled a handkerchief from his pocket and began polishing the top of the car. He wouldn't look at her and seemed intent on cleaning his entire vehicle before responding to her blunt statement. Colette decided to try another tactic before he had wiped the whole car down.

"Simo? Why do you want me to ride in the back seat of the car?"

Simo let out a breathy sigh of relief, there was something positively feminine about the man even though his bulk was considerable. "Thank you, Miss Colette. You're the employer and if you ride in the front, it will just confuse people. I don't want anyone to think that you are my girlfriend." Suddenly, as he realized his mistake. His bushy black eyebrows shot up, and his black eyes came to meet hers. She tried (for some reason) to look disapproving, but it hardly seemed necessary. Simo was in a tailspin.

"I mean it's not that you aren't beautiful. I mean, you are very beautiful, yes, very sexy—I mean not sexy. I wouldn't say sexy. It's not that I want to have sex with you, but it's—you know there is this thing with Moroccan men—I - they - we - but not really me, just them. I would be very honored to have you as my girlfriend or wife, but what I really mean is that—well, you know—like the king. It's like the king."

Despite herself, Colette was even more charmed and amused than she had been a moment before. Watching the man go from washing the car with his handkerchief to unconsciously proposing marriage to a woman he'd just met was not only telling about the personality of Simo, but perhaps it told her something of Moroccan men in general. She would need to be careful in this country—it seemed. Once again, she felt lucky to have found him rather than some more-polished version of a Moroccan macho man.

Simo had just given her a first lesson in Moroccan mentality. Authority and power were keys in the relationships between people here, and it would be very wise for her to remember that while she tried to restore her house and figure out what exactly she intended to do with it.

"Simo. Take a deep breath. Stop talking. I'll ride in the back." She stepped into the door he still held open and sat down inside the Mercedes. The interior was brightly colored upholstery that was very obviously not original. On the dashboard a red, white, and black striped carpet had been folded and a number of odd plastic animal figurines were carefully placed in a kind of vehicular diorama. A compact disc with a shoelace through the hole hung from the rearview mirror, and Arabic script had been written on both sides of it. The car smelled vaguely of cigarette smoke, but also had the aromatic smell of cinnamon and cardamom.

Simo closed the door behind her and walked around the back of the vehicle to reach the driver's seat. Opening the driver door, he sank into position and turned the key in the ignition. The car started smoothly, and Colette was happy to suspect that Simo took as good care of the engine as he did of the paint job.

"Simo, what was that you were saying about the king?" Colette had followed most of what he had been stammering, but the last bit was a little disconnected from the rest. She wanted to understand better, and since they had a long drive ahead of them, this was probably the best way to go about things.

"Oh, our King? His name is Mohammad Six, and he is really the best man in the world. We love the king. All Moroccans love him. If there were an election, he would certainly be the only candidate, and he would win by a huge margin."

Colette wasn't sure if his statement had made her think what he wanted her to think, but suspected her own Western ideas had read something into it.

"How does he rule?" She asked.

Simo considered for a moment and then embarked upon a long explanation of how the King of Morocco led his nation.

"Our King is like the father in a family, Miss Colette. He holds everything together and takes care of us. He builds hospitals and schools, and he will often make associations for people who don't have enough money. On our holidays, we wait for him to kill the first sheep or to lead us in our prayers, and he makes sure that Allah doesn't forget the Moroccan people.

"We are like his children, but he has many wives, and each wife is a different city, so the King has palaces in all of his favorite places. People are often trying to get him to come and stay in their cities, but of course, he can't stay in every city all the time, so we work hard to get his approval."

"Does he have a palace in Sefrou?" Colette asked. Sefrou was the nearest urban area to Sanhaja. It was where Simo was from.

Simo had a look of embarrassment in his eyes as they met hers in the rear-view mirror.

"No, there are some businessmen who have donated land near the taxi stand so the King can come and build a villa in Sefrou. He came to our city three years ago, and it was the first time a king had been there since his father cursed Sefrou in the

1960's so things are going to change very quickly. Once the King's palace is completed in Sefrou..."

"Wait a minute, Simo. You can't just say something like that and not explain it any further. His father cursed Sefrou?" If she hadn't stopped him, he would have just glossed over that.

Simo began to back-pedal. "Oh, no, I mean Hassan Thani was the father of Sefrou too. I mean he wouldn't have cursed it, but he was upset so he felt like he had to curse it." He took a breath. "Maybe I should explain a little more about Sefrou."

"Sefrou used to be called the Garden of Morocco. When King Hassan was a boy, his father would bring him to Sefrou for the Cherry Festival in the summer. It was their ancestor, Moulay Idriss who built Sefrou. It is the oldest walled city in Morocco. Moulay Idriss was the first Moroccan King. He chose Sefrou because, just like paradise, it had seven streams running through it. The ground was so fertile that you could simply drop the seeds upon it, and they would immediately begin to grow.

"So, Hassan Thani and his father, when they returned from Exile in France, they began to do all the important work of cleaning up the country and setting up a capital in Rabat. The French had built big, beautiful villas in Sefrou, and they had put a Moroccan Army garrison there to protect the city and keep things orderly. When the French left after independence, the Moroccan Army stayed in Sefrou, but many people began to take the villas for themselves. Also, the Yahoudi were going to Israel and that left a lot of places empty, and many Berbers began to move in."

Colette had to interrupt again. "What are Yahoudi, Simo?"

"Oh, sorry. Yahoudi. The Jews. Sefrou had more Jews than anywhere else in all of Africa, but when Israel became a state, they all moved away and abandoned their houses and farms. So, the French and then the Jews — they all left. It was more than half the population. The people who came to move into their houses were mostly Berber tribes, but also some people from other towns who heard they could move into nice houses for nothing. I don't mean to say they weren't as good as the French and the Yahoudi, but they weren't educated. They weren't craftsmen, artisans, or scholars like those who had left, and they didn't take care of Sefrou."

"Okay, so what about the King? Was it King Hassan?" Colette asked.

"Yes. After the death of his father, Mohammad Cinq, King Hassan came to Sefrou, and I think he was going to build a palace here. Some people say he thought of moving his capital here because of his memories of being here as a boy and his ancestor Moulay Idris. But, instead, he found that the new people who had moved in had polluted the river, built ugly houses, and destroyed his memories of the place. He was very unhappy."

"So, he cursed the city?" Colette asked.

"Well—yes. He cursed the people and the city for turning the Garden of Morocco into the ugliest town in Morocco. He moved the army base out of Sefrou so he would never have to see the city again, and he built his palace and university in Ifrane, which is now one of the richest cities in Morocco. It really should have been Sefrou."

"Wow. And no one came back until the new king?"

"That's right," Simo said. "The older people came out as he walked through the streets, and they cried and begged forgiveness and thanked him for his mercy in returning. So, now, people are pretty sure that Sefrou is going to come back."

"And the King is going to build a palace there?"

Simo shook his head, contradicting his own earlier statement. "No, I think those are just lies. You can't trust anything a Moroccan tells you because they are only trying to trick you into believing they are more important than they really are. The King might come back to Sefrou, but to be honest, it is just getting more ruined all the time. We have a cherry festival every year, but the cherries don't grow there anymore because people cut down all the cherry trees to build cheap houses. We have to bring cherries from Ifrane now. I don't think the King is going to leave Ifrane. It's like Switzerland there, and he has some problems and

70

needs to be out of the heat. But, the King is really wonderful, Miss Colette. He makes all the rules of our society, and he is one of the richest men in the world. He's like the Bill Gates of Morocco."

"But Bill Gates invented Windows and created Microsoft—did the King invent something?" Colette couldn't help being a bit annoyed when it came to wealth and power worship.

"I'm sure he must have, Miss Colette. He's the king."

Driving Miss Colette

Chapter 7: Driving Miss Colette

As one would expect, Colette had done some research about Morocco before hopping on the plane, and she wasn't completely ignorant about the country, the monarchy, the customs, or the culture. Yes, there were some dramatic holes in her knowledge—like what the King looked like—but they would be filled by her boots on the ground. Nothing can prepare you for a place before you actually go there.

Leaving the airport, she felt like she could be in the South of France. The land around the airport looked like any small-town airport in the States, but once they turned away from the modern construction and infrastructure, the first of many shocks was seeing a man in a tan djellaba riding sidesaddle on a tiny donkey. The donkey was shaggy and miserable looking with long gray fur and a terribly sad, long face. The man sitting on the donkey looked positively bored as the little beast under him trotted along. The donkey couldn't have weighed much more than the man, but the little beast didn't seem to be straining under the burden.

A woven straw basket hung to the side of the donkey. It was filled with tree branches and fodder. Perhaps the donkey was carrying his own lunch with him. Colette didn't know if donkeys ate branches or not. The landscape looked vastly more ancient than she had expected from arriving at the modern, new airport, but modern airports are rarely in the midst of the cities they serve, so she wasn't surprised as the rural landscape faded, and concrete buildings rose on either side of the highway.

Concrete was definitely the number one building material in Morocco. It seemed generally to be left unpainted, though some of the modern buildings were painted with either a brick-red or an off-tone, dull yellow color. The color brought to mind pee-stained toilet seats, not an image she wanted to keep in her mind or ever have to think about. The keys to the riad were secured in her bag which Simo had placed in the trunk before placing her in the back seat.

"Miss Colette. Would you mind if I turned on some music?" Simo asked, taking his eyes from the road for a hectic moment.

"Yes, of course," she said, frantically motioning to him that he should put his eyes back on the road.

Simo turned back towards the front and began to fiddle with the radio. From what she could see, he was still not looking at the road, but veered just in time to avoid hitting an entire family that suddenly loomed ahead of them in a brightly painted red and blue three wheeled motorbike truck. Jumping around the stations, Simo settled on one that to Colette's ears sounded like a couple of women had screamed into a digital recording device, slightly delayed one track, sped up another track, and had someone who didn't know how to play the violin record another track without

74

listening to the screaming women. Next, the engineers must have dubbed in some distortion. On the blown-out speakers of the Mercedes it was a combination of yowling cats and fingernails on chalkboards.

Simo obviously didn't feel the same way because his head began to bob happily to the music, and she could see a smile and contented look on his chubby face.

The music fit the environment Colette saw rolling by outside and gradually she was able to begin understanding the melodic qualities of it. Moroccan music was like nothing she had ever heard, and it took some getting used to. Chalky, white-washed hovels made of cardboard, rusty tin, and concrete sat next to huge luxury apartment buildings, classic old art-deco buildings without maintenance for decades rotted away while residents occupied them with seemingly unconcerned abandon. Skin hues ranged from Canada white to Congo black, all-in bright headscarves and geometric patterned robes, one people, all trudging alongside the highway. Often it was only the scarves that distinguished the women from the men in their form hiding djellabas. Colette had no idea how one might identify the association of their tribe or region. She was, however, surprised to see women with their heads uncovered in Casablanca and even more surprised when a deep brown girl in a mini-skirt and a head scarf whizzed by them on a high powered vespa.

"Simo...?" She wanted to ask him about the women and head covering, but the music was too loud, and as she looked at his happily bobbing head, she decided it was better to let him concentrate on the road.

As they passed through the city of Casablanca, Colette felt no desire to stop and visit it. It was—the White City, the city of North African romance—but truly it looked like a squalid slum. A mist of smog and heavy traffic veering from the freeway towards the city told her what she would find there. A steady stream of motorbikes, donkey carts, and djellaba-covered bicycle riders had position on either side of the road, and the tin roofed shanties weighed down with tires, broken bricks, rocks, and old metal scrap to keep the roofs from blowing off told her enough.

A massive minaret rose in the distance, and she could see the waters of the Atlantic sparkling behind it. It was hard to believe that New York was across that water. This was more like being on a different planet or traveling through time than like taking a comfortable flight to a modern country. Yetet, the billboards beside the highway showed iPhones with pretty-looking Arab girls gazing transfixed at the latest apps and happy-looking Arab families eating Dannon yogurt in ultra-modern kitchens. She was happy that none of them said "Lordy, Lordy, Colette Forty!"

All that she saw was in stark contrast, when held against the countless small flocks of almost feral looking sheep and goats they now began to pass. They were tended by guys that might just as well have been Peruvian Indians hunkered down in their faded work coats with deeply worn faces. A scenic river wound under the highway on one side—on the other side—a huge landfill of garbage flown over by flocks of green, blue, purple, black, and white plastic bags. The bags held formation with the many gulls that were drawn to human refuse. A big bulldozer pushed an avalanche of garbage towards the bank of the river where it tumbled down and choked it with rubbish and debris that instantly turned the clear water from one side to a toxic looking orange-red sludge. There were dozens of people scouring the rubbish for anything that might be able to provide even a moment's relief from the abject hunger and poverty they lived in.

The car now carried them into a landscape more pastoral with big cypress trees rising to either side of the road and sometimes blocking the view of the countless hovels and shacks around them. Modern pedestrian crossing bridges were ignored by scarf-covered gaggles of girls and women who darted through fast-moving cars and trucks rather than carrying their loads up the stairs to the safer pedestrian walkway. Colette had known that Morocco would be a land of contrasts, but her underestimation had been as vast as the gap between rich and poor. The cat screeching music and the rhythm of the road had a hypnotic effect and despite a keen interest in seeing where she was going, her eyelids closed like drawbridges of a fairy tale castle, and she soon entered the blissful land of sleep.

The Dream Master

Chapter 8: Meeting the Dream Master

The car droned over the highway. Colette's sleep deepened, no longer was she the self of this waking world. No longer was she that proud and gold-obsessed slave creating fierce golden jewelry for self-absorbed socialites who were as unaware of their own motivations as they were moved like pawns on a world-sized game board. She was transported beyond the cloying smell of the spice bazaar to a swirling mist of colors, shapes, textures, and smells weaving their way from one world to another and another. No longer simply in and of Morocco, but not necessarily in or about anywhere else either. The sound of the trance, the smell of the feelings, each just one more thread woven into the pattern of her sleeping life force and suddenly no longer in the car and unaware, but instead a girl on a road near a house where she now faded in and found herself someplace entirely different.

The feel of the wool djellaba was coarse against her skin, and the silk scarf caressed her face where it spilled from being wrapped over her hair. The tactile-sensory projecting machine that her brain had become went into overdrive. The little donkey jounced and pranced under her, and his surprisingly soft fur soothed her exhausted hands as she stroked him—not for him, but for her. Pierre, the donkey's big head swiveled to look at her with an appraising look, though she had not spoken his name aloud. The edges of a smile glimmered on Pierre's donkey lips before the big head turned back forward, leaving the impression that one of those huge mournful brown eyes had winked at her.

Pierre's hooves clip clopped as they made their way on the hard, cobbled road but became silent as he stepped into the sand. In short order, they began winding their way through a maze of towering dunes. The hump of his back was padded over with a large woolen blanket, and his long tan neck stretched towards the sun beating down from overhead amidst the deepest blue skies she had ever seen. As she sat in the basket, the motion of the donkey-turned-camel caused her to sway and groove, and the song of the Berber nomads who stood on the dunes above made her feel confident that Pierre had never actually changed, only her perception of him had.

Kneeling so she could easily get off, Pierre swept the top hat from his head and motioned her forward with a bow. And she wondered at how she had forgotten half of his name for so long and mentally *appellated* his second name on the first. Pierre-Antoine. He turned and walked back into the desert from which they had just emerged. She watched him struggle up the dunes—an old man in the desert—his walking stick creating a third track paired with his feet. Time stood still as he shrank in the distance until he disappeared from sight first and then also from mind.

Colette stood alone surrounded by the desert wilds. A black tent made of old blankets strung on a round-pointed frame stood in front of her. Two women motioned her inside, and she was not surprised they were her mother and Destiny standing on either side of the doorway.

"Destiny!" Colette said brightly, happy to see her radiant friend.

"Shhh. You're not supposed to see me, Girl. He's waiting for you. Go inside." Destiny spoke with an unsettlingly crisp British accent. It fit her perfectly despite being false. How was the wrong able to feel so right? Destiny motioned her through the doors.

Her mother, as would be expected wherever she might be, had the final word. "Take your time and make sure that you carry your ancestors on your sleeve. Oh, and Colette, do be a lady about things. This isn't just some silly tea party. It's important."

Colette ducked through the tent flaps, and the two women dropped them behind her. The interior was darker than she had expected so she paused to allow her eyes a moment to adjust to the sudden change from blinding light to blinding dark. It was an immense space considering how small the tent had looked from outside. In front of her was a large wooden desk covered with papers and books. This was the workspace of a field marshal or a general at war—a place where lives were decided and battles were won or lost. A single candle's flame danced on her right creating shadows that taunted merrily the corners of her eyes. As her vision stabilized and returned to her the power of depth, she experienced the slow discovery of a man looking at her from behind the desk. His long white beard wound among the papers he was working with. He ignored her, and soon his quill pen scratched unintelligible marks on a scroll unrolled in front of him. To his left, an ink bottle. To his right, a massive ring of keys. The brightness of his djellaba now lit the room. She dared not disturb him for his authority shone brighter even than the Sahara day she had so recently left behind. He labored over his composition, oblivious to her presence.

Finally, he raised his head. The winds of a thousand years sailed forth from his eyes and pierced her bones to the marrow. He frowned. She felt herself on the verge of a good old-fashioned scolding. Everyone else had been so nice to her since she had entered this realm that she found it to be a bit of a shock. The look on his face was now one of disgust. He turned to the left side and spat on the floor before turning to regard her again.

"I would ask you about your beliefs, but you don't seem to have any." He said it with contempt.

"That's not true," Colette returned. "I believe many things. I believe in destiny."

"Fine," he spat again. "Tell me about your belief in God."

"I don't believe in God," Colette told him. "I think God is a manufactured control system created by men to control women—and other men."

His laughter echoed into the dark hollows of the Earth. The soft walls of the tent now a rough and hard stone radiating the cold, jeering voice into a chorus of mockery. She wanted to run. She wanted to get away. She wanted to wake up. The realization that she was in a dream came suddenly and with it a sense of power returned to her. Yet, she could not go; he would not let her, even if she tried.

"Who are you to claim there is no God? Do you think yourself so much better than all of those who believe?"

"That's not it. They are not my concern. They worship something, of that I have no doubt, but I don't think that they are worshiping what they think they are. That's all, it's just my opinion. I don't have proof, but I need more than books and the belief of others."

He picked up the keys allowing the scroll in front of him to roll itself closed. "Each of the keys is a window to a portion of the divine. Don't you realize you have already been put on the path that will lead you to your own soul? The moment you chose the keys, you chose the life you are heading towards, and whether you chose them or they were able to choose you—you are now an instrument of their journey. With great power flowing about so freely, do you think there is no one responsible for it?"

Colette looked at the holy man. Who was he? Had she just told a pope that there was no God? Having labeled him, his image coalesced more closely into that of a pope. A warm breeze wrapped around her before escaping through his chamber window. The scroll upon which he had been writing lifted from among his jumble and slowly approached her. No hand or visible force controlled it. She reached her hand towards it, and just short of the hand reaching the scroll, it tumbled to the ground in front of her. She knelt, grasped it, and rose again. Her intent was to put it back on his desk, but things had changed, and now he was a man black. The desk was clear of any papers at all. She didn't want to put it there. Everything in her screamed not to.

"You are heading to a place that is both sad and triumphant. Sad in that the people who built it loved it, created traditions in it, worshiped in it, and loved in it—were forced to leave and have never come back to see it again. Triumphant in that it has found in you, a new caretaker and one who shall be trusted, in time, with all of the secrets that lie within. The arcane lessons of time will be laid before you—if you allow them to be. There is no reason to fear, for what is lost is never completely gone, and that which is found is never found completely. Give up what you fear losing and suddenly it is no longer worth fearing." He looked up and she looked with him.

There was nothing to see, but when she looked back down, he had changed again. "Curious, the situation is," the black pope had become Yoda. "The force one thinks is missing, but missing from the force is one. The force then upon one puts the force." She blinked.

The man, for he was again ancient, his long white beard nearly reaching the ground. No desk in front of him now. He turned and walked into the corner where he began to chant in Arabic and make mysterious gestures with his long fingers in the shadows against the wall of the tent. Wisps of incense smoke rose to form billowy clouds of ancient symbols.

Colette was stretched out on the back seat of the car. Chanting sura from the blown out speakers felt far more powerful at a far more reasonable volume than it had before. She could see white clouds in the blue sky above as the car hurtled toward her destiny, heading directly toward her future. She just wasn't sure exactly what that future was.

Yoda. It must have been the sandwich she ate on the plane.

New Eyes

Chapter 9: New Eyes

All the research in the world can't really prepare you for the shock of Morocco. Colette was rapidly learning that this was a land of contrasts. A massive telecom billboard next to what looked like an ancient mud pueblo, a black window-tinted BMW next to a Berber on a donkey, a woman in the full veil wearing Louis Vuitton sunglasses with not an inch of her skin showing and two minutes later a girl in a backless blouse with long brown legs in short pants astraddle and bare over a motor scooter.

It was hard to believe that the Jewish people of Morocco had felt such a compulsion to leave—this seemed to be a land of vast tolerance though, as they progressed further away from the sea, she saw a marked increase in the number of mosque minarets rising from village after village. In some cases, the minaret stood alone surrounded by fields, and she wondered why they had chosen to build in such locations. Frequently, she saw white-washed mud-brick buildings with green tile roofs in prominent locations—on a hillside, next to a stream, beside a grove. There was something odd about them. No windows, not necessarily a mosque since many of them had no minarets, but they didn't look like homes either.

Simo was still happily listening to the droning chant of prayers over the car's tape deck, and she had to tap him on the shoulder to get his attention. He turned to her—.

"Keep watching the road," she snapped and then instantly regretted it. She felt like she'd just kicked a happy child. "What is this you're listening to now, Simo? Is it poetry?" It was either poetry, prayers, or both, but she couldn't imagine anyone just listening to prayers on a cassette the way they might listen to the Rolling Stones or a U2 Album.

Obviously straining not to turn and face her when he spoke, he said "It's Sura, Miss Colette." And then when she waited for more, he didn't say anything else—as if he expected her to recognize the name.

"Sura? Is that a famous poet? A singer? What's Sura, Simo?"

He giggled. "Sura Simo. That would be a funny name." He turned towards her again with a big grin, but seeing her face remembered himself and snapped his head back to the front. "You don't know Sura?" He sounded amazed. "These are the words of the Quran as they were written by the Prophet Mohammad, Peace Be Upon Him. They are recited by those with the most understanding or the most beautiful voices. Personally, I like the Egyptian reciters much more than the Saudi reciters, but I'm not a purist."

He even talked about the verses as if he were talking about music or poetry. So interesting.

"And what about these little white buildings we see from time to time?" They were passing another one, and she pointed to it.

Simo looked at her in the mirror with obvious disapproval in his eyes. "Oh, it's better not to even notice those," he said. Which of course wasn't even close to the answer she wanted and just excited a cat-like curiosity in her that wouldn't rest until she knew more.

"What are they, Simo?" She tried to sound nice though she wanted to strangle him all of a sudden.

"Well, some people say that they are the tombs of saints and holy men. People go to worship them so that they can have the saints carry their prayers to God and get them help for the things they need in their lives. My mother says that they are filled with the bones of donkeys and are a joke played by djinn and Shaitan on stupid people—if you worship donkey bones, you are going to go to hell for sure."

Colette tried to process all of that but was having a hard time getting past the last part. 'If you worship donkey bones, you're going to hell for sure.' It was said in about the same tone as a five-year-old American kid might say, "If you don't wash the dishes, Santa won't bring you any presents." Simo's mom, Colette decided that she would have to meet this woman, though the thought for some reason made her nervous to think about.

"So, they are like chapels or temples?" Colette still wanted to understand the little structures.

"No, they are tombs. I mean people say they are tombs, but like I said, my mom..."

Colette cut him off before he could continue. "You can tell me about your mom another time, but I want to know what people in general say about them. They are tombs of holy men?"

Simo again looked back with disapproving eyes in his heavy cheeks and round baby face. "Right. People go to them to get baraka." Colette was picturing people getting cookies at the tombs, but then realized she was seeing baklava in her mind.

"What is baraka?" she asked.

"Really? You don't know baraka either? Okay. Baraka is kind of hard to explain. We all have two angels on our shoulders that record good and bad deeds, and when we die, they get weighed to see where we go. If you have baraka, it makes the bad deeds lighter."

"So, Baraka is good deeds?"

"No. Baraka is baraka. You can get baraka from going to pray at a saint's tomb or touching a holy person, or sometimes people can give you baraka when you make them a meal or are a very good guest or host. It's not good or bad, it just makes your bad deeds lighter. But all of that is really magic kind of stuff and my mother says..."

"Simo, can we stop at a temple thingy?" Colette asked him.

He looked confused. "What's a temple thingy?"

"One of the tombs. Can we stop at one?"

"Oh, it's okay, we have some in Sefrou. We have one of the most famous and beautiful ones at the Monument, and then there are plenty around. Don't worry, you'll get to see them, but I don't really want to stop at them. My mother says that you can pick up djinn that way."

"You mean genies?"

"No, I mean djinn. They live in other worlds, but they come out at the tombs because of the people worshiping them. My mom says that the people are actually worshiping djinn at the tombs. They also come through the drains and love empty houses. Don't worry though Miss Colette, we're going to spray black chicken blood on your walls and pour salt down your drains before you move into your house."

Colette just let that one go, it was too much. Apparently, he didn't want to stop and actually it would be good to get to Sefrou and then to Sanhaja.

"What time will we get to Sefrou, Simo?"

He didn't say anything.

"Simo. What time do we get to Sefrou?" If it had been anyone else, she might have begun having thoughts of kidnapping and terrorists but with Simo, she just couldn't believe that was possible. "Simo."

As if an idea had just come into his head—Simo immediately brightened. "You're very lucky, Miss Colette. It's not very often that people get to come to a Moroccan wedding on their first day in Morocco."

A sinking feeling pulsed through her body—was she being married off and sold into white slavery? What about her house? When would she get to see her house?

"What wedding, Simo? No one said anything about a wedding. I want to get to my house in Sanhaja."

"Oh, you don't want to miss this, Miss Colette. My brother is marrying a Fassi girl, and she comes from a very rich family so there is a big party in Fes. All of my family and friends are there, and we're going to get to Fes just about in time for the food to be served. I checked with my mom, and she said you can come as a guest of the family. You are Welcome in Morocco, Miss Colette."

"Simo, I don't have anything to wear. I'm tired and want to have a shower—"

"Oh, don't worry Miss Colette, my sisters and cousins will take very good care of you. They have plenty of kaftans, and you can have a shower later. Don't worry, you look fine."

There wasn't really any way to get out of it. She had already learned one of the most important lessons in Morocco— you can't escape a wedding invitation.

The Lovers

Chapter 10: The Lovers

Crap. A wedding. She knew a Moroccan wedding was going to be different from some New York socialite event, but then Simo had said that the bride's family was wealthy. It might not be that different after all. She hadn't really packed anything that was suitable to wear, but Simo said she would be taken care of. There was a part of her that wanted to insist that he just take her to Sanhaja and let her skip the wedding, but another part of her knew that was just the tiredness of jetlag and the little bit of bitchiness that came along with it.

It was his older brother's wedding, and she'd be damned if she was going to be the reason why he missed it. Besides, this was a first chance to see what this country was really about and to discover something unique and beautiful. Furthermore, she was a jewelry designer, and every woman there would be wearing her best pieces—she could expect to find huge inspiration, perhaps meet some important people who would make her life in Morocco better, and finally, she would have the chance to meet Simo's mother who seemed to be the person he admired more than anyone. Again, she had a vague, ill-at-ease feeling at the thought of it, but discounted that for nerves.

It was this aspect of her personality that had made her successful at nearly everything she had done. A situation came up that wasn't necessarily what she wanted, and she looked for opportunity in it rather than bemoaning her fate and beating her metaphorical head against the wall.

"They live in the medina qadima, the old city, so we're going to have to park the car and walk down to their riad. It's not far, don't worry."

"Simo, what about my bags?" The last thing she needed was for her luggage to be stolen on the first day she was here.

"Don't worry about that Miss Colette. I'm going to pay someone to watch over the car while we're gone. If you need to bring anything, we can take it with us."

She did a quick mental calculation. She had most of the make-up she might need in her handbag, and even if she were to go through her bag, there wasn't much in the way of wedding attire in it. She'd brought a fair number of things to work in, but not much in the way of dressing-up clothes, since she'd known, she was going to a village in the countryside. There was a pair of spiky black heels that she'd brought with her just on the off chance that something did come up—you could always find nice clothing, but a pair of nice shoes—it was always better to bring them with you. Those and a gold lamé scarf were really all she had to work with. She hoped that Simo's family really would be able to outfit her. She didn't want to be the sore thumb in the crowd of revelers.

Driving into Fez took her breath away. High crumbling walls and ramparts winding around the hillsides. Massive mud-block buildings and wide tree lined avenues that seemed to contain nothing, but cafes filled with dark skinned, dark haired men drinking coffee or tea that matched their complexions— everything from cafe crème to cafe noir. There was also plenty of golden colored tea with bright green leaves stuffed into the clear glasses. There were guidebook wielding tourists strolling down the boulevard, but for the most part, Fez seemed to be populated by locals—which made sense but wasn't exactly what she had expected.

"This is the Ville-Nouvelle," Simo told her. "The French didn't want to live in the old medina, so they built a modern city outside of it. Lots of people hated the French, but really, I'm glad they came because otherwise there probably wouldn't be any medina left at all. Fez's Medina is the largest car-free urban area in the world, and it's the best preserved of all the ancient Islamic cities."

Colette wasn't sure about the veracity of Simo's patois, but it sounded feasible. As they crested the hill and began their way down to the medina, she lost all of her doubts. Stretching before her was an endless sea of mud brick buildings crammed together so tightly that it was probably impossible for a car to get through them. Passing through a massive arch, she could see the ruins of what looked like a castle on the hillside which had just been lit as the sun was beginning to sink below the hills to the west. She could see the lights of the medina twinkling on as if some giant hand of God were creating the constellation.

She rolled down the window, and at that moment the call to prayer began. There were perhaps thousands of mosques in Fez from what she could see, and the call warbled at her from every direction. The Imams were not perfectly coordinated in their cadence nor in their timing, but the overlapping waves of the words reached her like waves from the seven seas rushing at an island in the midst of them. Each hitting her shore, bouncing off, creating new waves, and then coming back for more. Even in the car, she had the sense that something magnificent was happening, and as they came to a stop at a huge car park filled with city buses on one side and crumbling city walls on the other, she hopped out of the back seat and stood entranced by the sounds, her skin goosing up with tiny bumps and a prickling sensation feathering its way up and down her spine. As the last echoes faded out, she turned to where Simo had gotten out of the car and leaned against the rooftop of the old Mercedes.

"It's easy to see why this is the spiritual capital of Morocco, isn't it Miss Colette?"

She had no words. She had no need to say anything.

A crusty old man with a face like a thousand-year-old piece of leather came shuffling up. His bright yellow vest was the only

thing that told Colette he wasn't coming to beg for change. Simo
gave the man some coins from his pocket as the two of them
exchanged greetings. "Salaam alaikum." Peace upon you. "Wa
alaikum a salaam." And upon you peace. They were the only
words Colette knew in Arabic, and she kicked herself for not using
them when she greeted Simo and reminded herself to make sure
to say it to everyone else, she met through her day.

"You can grab what you need from the trunk, Miss
Colette. The guardian will watch over the car while we're gone."
The word guardian sounded so massive when compared to the
little man with his four teeth and big empty grin, but she supposed
he knew what he was doing. She pulled the heels and scarf from
her suitcase and stuffed them into her purse. "Okay, lead the way
Kimosabi."

She had no idea why she'd just called Simo by the Lone
Ranger's affectionate term for his Native American sidekick and
trusted friend—or was it the other way around. Certainly, she felt
anxiety as she followed him into a dark alleyway. How in the
world had she gotten herself into this? Was it really just that she
had wanted to buy some old keys?

She followed Simo through an arched doorway and
entered a different world. The narrow alleyways were not wide
enough for cars. As they walked through, she noticed hundreds of
passages leading off into shadows, each one branching before she

could figure out exactly what direction it was supposed to go. The alley they were in was wide enough for three people to walk abreast.

"Look out!" Simo shoved her against a wall, and three donkeys loaded with Coke crates trotted past and around the corner in front of them. Wide enough for one loaded donkey and someone pressed against the wall—Colette took note.

It took about fifteen minutes and what seemed like thousands of years back in time among the twists and turns before they reached a huge wooden door with a brass knocker on it. The knocker was a hand extending downward and holding an orb. When Simo lifted the hand, and then let it drop, it sent a hollow sounding thunk through the wood and the alleyway they stood in. Just to make sure, Simo reached over and pushed a small white button which rang a chiming doorbell inside.

A smaller door built inside of the large door opened and a woman of immense circumference peeked her face from behind it. Her head was wrapped in a colorful silk scarf, and her initial look of distrust turned to delight upon seeing Simo.

'A salaam alaikum," and a lot of talking that sounded affectionate. The woman's actions matched her spirit and form as she rushed out and grabbed Simo making him look like a much smaller man than he really was. Colette heard a "Wa alaikum a salaam" from him, but the rest was muffled as he was crushed in the woman's embrace and smothered in kisses. The woman spoke a seemingly endless torrent of words that sounded like questions but gave no pause for answers. Finally, Simo managed to break away with a big smile on his face and turned to Colette.

"Miss Colette, this is my mom." He then introduced his mother to her in Arabic, and the woman turned her big eyes on Colette who now felt like a small girl being sized up by a new teacher. Apparently, the woman liked what she saw because she threw her log-like arms around her and pummeled her with the same question-sounding words she had barraged her son with. Her thick fleshy lips kissed either cheek on Colette's face repeatedly, and her warmth and welcome threatened to cause Colette to pass out from a lack of oxygen. Simo pulled his mother away.

"She wants to know all about you and where your husband is, what you are doing and all this stuff. I'll warn you now, she is already trying to figure out if she can marry you to me or one of my other brothers, but don't worry, that's just what Moroccan moms do. Please, come inside."

Simo seemed immediately at home, kicking off his shoes and accepting a cup of tea from another woman with big friendly eyes. He handed Colette a cup as she was led off by two more girls. Simo called out instructions to them in Arabic and then explained to Colette—"You are with my sister Fatima and my cousin Fatima-Zahara. They are going to help to get you ready."

As Colette looked over her shoulder, Simo was heading into a room filled with a combination of men in worn looking suits and men in beautiful djellabas and yellow Fezzes. The girls laughed and giggled, but neither of them seemed to know any English. They led her to a room filled with women and children.

All of the women wore the beautiful shiny gowns that would have been the envy of any prom. They were all doing up each other's hair and makeup while trying to keep the many kids who ran around from mucking up the place too badly. The kids wore a combination of western and Moroccan wear, just like the men, but the women were all Moroccan and looked like visions from an orientalist painting of the 19th century. Fatima and Fatima-Zahara led her to another girl who was busy doing a big curly hairdo on a tall, subdued woman.

The girl turned to Colette and smiled. "They've brought you to me because I'm the only one who speaks English. I'm Aziza." Aziza held out her hand. She had a similar accent to Simo's, but her English was much more British than his. "You might think that I'm just the hairdresser—but actually, I'm the bride."

Colette smiled and laughed. She liked this girl already. "Very pleased to meet you, Aziza. And congratulations. Is there anything I can do to help?" Colette didn't know what she could do, but she loved the fact that the bride was taking care of the other women, even as she was getting ready for one of the biggest moments of her life.

Aziza was wispy, willowy, probably around twenty-five years old—and had a long, fresh face that was brought to life by huge almond shaped eyes. Her eyes reflected everything going on around her in bottomless black pools that seemed to push out light and smiles in such a way that her face became radiant. Her sable hair was wrapped in a top-styled coif so thick and rich that if the pins were let loose, , the wavy strands would fall all the way to the floor. She had a smooth complexion and defined, dark eyebrows. This was Aziza's wedding day. She surely shined.

The room they sat in would have blown Colette's mind had her mind not already been completely blown away by Morocco. Walls of colorful blue, red, white, yellow, and black mosaic tiles carefully arranged into eight pointed stars and repetitive geometric patterns. Colette had to touch the walls to make sure that it wasn't patterns baked into the tiles because the pattern was so regular and uniform. How in the world had they done that? How long had it taken?

Overhead, massive cedar beams were carved and ran parallel to one another. The room was a long rectangle with another huge set of wooden doors that opened into a central courtyard bigger than most gardens in New York. The courtyard was filled with orange trees and tropical plants—heliconia flowers and birds of paradise burst out in startling arrays of color. Birds flitted from tree to plant and alighted on the edge of the fountain which merrily splashed in the exact center.

Above the tiles but below the ceiling was intricately carved plaster work that not only continued the geometric motifs but carried it further. Three massive light-filled lamps diffused through colored Iraqi stained glass filled the room with a multihued brightness, carrying the glow over the furniture and the women themselves.

The furniture was mostly low sedan sofas lining the walls all the way around. Massive, overstuffed velvet pillows of various shapes were stacked and piled, sometimes falling onto the floor in a cascade of silk and lace, mirroring the gowns the women wore.

The floor had yet more intricate tile work but was covered by beautiful hand-woven wool rugs. Various leather poofs and big octagonal tables completed the furnishings. That left the women themselves who were fluttering around like brightly colored butterflies, putting on, shedding, and examining the many brightly colored gowns that filled the room. The gowns seemed to be communal property, and if one was not being worn or being taken off, it seemed to be fair game. Women sat in small clusters arranging hair and makeup with Aziza sitting in the prime position in front of the lone stand-up mirror and make-up table. She was the star after all, and she filled the role perfectly.

"Okay, first you have to find a gown. There are lots of them here. Just go and see what strikes your fancy—with your skin, I would probably stay away from yellow or pink, those go better with darker tones. In fact, the darker the gown you can find, the better it will look." Aziza turned back towards the mirror and the woman whose hair she was carefully filling with glitter.

Colette bumped into a slim woman who had the most captivating eyes she had ever seen. They were wide and big like an anime character, but nearly three times as long as they were wide. Her pupils were the largest Colette had ever seen. The girl hissed at her as she reached down to pick up a package she had dropped "Humara gabi"—and then she was off but not before shooting lightning rods of hate from those big, beautiful eyes at both Colette and Aziza.

Aziza laughed. "Don't worry about her, that was Jamila— she hates me because she wants my man, and I won't let her have him. Now, go get yourself a dress—you can't stand there all day."

There was a black gown that suited her perfectly, but Colette wouldn't wear black to a wedding. She wasn't too superstitious, but she knew that you don't wear black, and you don't wear white. Instead, she found a dark royal blue kaftan that wrapped around her like a second skin and made her feel as if she were at home with the paradise of butterfly women who surrounded her. And she couldn't help wondering what the men were doing.

Then, suddenly, all the women were changing out of the nice kaftans and back into much more regular clothing. What in the world was happening?

"Aziza? What's happening?" She found the girl now wearing jeans and a djellaba-like blouse. She had a powder blue scarf wrapped over her head.

"It's time to go eat," Aziza said. "We don't want to get stains on the gowns."

It was a day of firsts for Colette and the Moroccan Wedding Feast was yet another. She was glad they had come. The women moved into the central courtyard, through the garden and into another large rectangular room. This one was set with low tables and cushions on the floor.

"My mother likes to do things the old-fashioned way," Aziza explained.

The women gathered around the tables and sat in groups talking and laughing. Colette noticed Jamila sitting at a table of very beautiful girls. They were also chatting and laughing but seemed far less happy. There was something about the way they looked around at everyone as if they wanted to be seen having a better time than the others. And that thought led to another.

"Where are the men? Aren't they going to eat with us?"

Aziza translated the question into Arabic before answering, and the women at the table laughed and feigned shock. They were mostly middle-aged women though some were far older, presumably Aziza's aunt's and friends of her mother. Aziza had told her that her mother would be there soon.

"We eat separately from the men so they can't see how much better the food we make for ourselves is," she translated that again and it brought peals of laughter from the women. One or two of them giving a disapproving 'Hashuma!' while continuing to laugh. "Actually, it's just custom. Adil and I wanted to have a more modern wedding where the guests eat together, but my mother—I told you; she likes the old-fashioned ways. So, the men are next door having their meal and enjoying their time together, and we get to have a little party of our own without the men to distract us."

Colette felt silly for asking but needed to make sure. "Adil is your husband?"

Aziza laughed. "Not yet, but he will be soon. Of course, Jamilla and the evil sisters might still have some sort of tricks they try to pull."

"But why did you invite them if they don't like you?"

Aziza looked very serious. "I don't know how it is in your country, but here, you have to invite your sister to your wedding." Colette could see it now. The two girls were very different, but the eyes were the same, though more pronounced on Jamila. How awful that must be.

The food, however, was not awful. Far from it.

The meal began with a girl of around fourteen and a younger girl of about twelve coming around with a pitcher of warm water and a basin. Each of the women held out their hands over the basin and water was poured on them. This was followed by soap and then after a good wash, a rinse with more warm water. The girl with the basin also had a towel which she handed to each guest when they were done.

Roasted chicken served with apricots and lots and lots of bread. Big oval loaves that were only about an inch high but were broken up into dozens of pieces and distributed by the women at the table. There were no forks being used, though someone had brought one and handed it to Colette. She figured, when in Rome you should do as the Romans do, so she also ate with her hands, albeit more delicately than the Moroccan women around her. Their method was to reach into the big dishes on the center of the table, use one hand to hold down a chicken and the other to rip the piece of it off that they wanted to eat. Their hands were covered in the chicken juice and none of them seemed to care. Colette looked around for napkins but didn't see any. Someone had put a towel on her lap, and she used it to wipe her hands, though she felt slightly guilty doing so.

Next came the drinks. Young boys brought tea, Coke, and Fanta in large bottles and offered it to the guests. The soft drinks were poured into tea glasses. There was also an orange soda called Hawaii which seemed curiously out of place here but also seemed popular with the older women. Colette had tea and upon the first sip realized that there was more sugar in it than if she had taken the Coke.

A second course followed. Lamb with prunes—the process of eating it was roughly the same and while the chicken had been delicious, the lamb was even better. Colette was surprised by the sweetness of all the food since she'd really been expecting more of a savory flavor—couscous, cinnamon, and olives—but this meal certainly had limited amounts of those elements.

Finally, after a leisurely hour of devouring meat, the final course was brought—a fruit plate with dates, orange slices, and cherries. This was followed by another round of the hand washing girls, thankfully. At this point the women were all leaning back on their hands and relaxing like fat old uncles in New York who had stuffed themselves at a Thanksgiving feast. Colette had been astounded at how much some of them had been able to put away and at times had felt like perhaps it was the only meal they were going to have for the next weeks. Looking around at the happy plump women that surrounded her though, she knew that wasn't going to be the case. She would have to watch her figure while she was here. If this meal were any indication, sugar and bread were the main staples.

It was approaching 7 pm, but none of the women, including Aziza, seemed in any hurry to get back in their wedding attire. They sat around in small groups chatting and laughing, resting after the big meal. In some cases, taking naps with rugs or blankets pulled up over them. Colette couldn't imagine what the men were doing, but it seemed that the hen party happened immediately prior to the wedding. This being an Islamic country, there was no alcohol which probably was what made it possible. No need to recover the next day from too much wine, also no way to calm the nerves prior to the big moment.

Finally, there was a visible sign that this was a wedding when Simo and Adil's mom appeared with her mascara running down her face. She was weeping as though she were at a funeral rather than a wedding, and none of the other older ladies seemed capable of calming her down. It was, surprisingly, Jamila who came to the rescue and hugged the older woman tightly. She finally calmed and then went over to where Aziza was now starting to get up in preparation for getting ready. Jamila stood back with a small smile on her face, it was a human smile, not the sort of mask that Colette expected. Simo's mom—*I will have to learn her name at some point*, Colette thought—began talking gently to Aziza, primping her, checking her hair, and sometimes simply looking at her. Then, suddenly, she was embracing her and weeping again. There was some serious drama going on here, but since it was all in Arabic, Colette didn't understand a bit of the language—but the emotion came through clearly. Aziza was now her daughter.

The drama was a signal for the women to move back across the courtyard to the ready room again. Kaftans, gowns, and heavy eye make-up ('kohl' was the word Aziza called it)—a sort of black powder that might well have been charcoal powder. This didn't feel so much like a wedding as a fashion show, and it was 11 pm before anything happened that might indicate a wedding was underway.

From outside came the sound of a buzzing klaxon horn and what sounded like the banging together of garbage can lids. To Colette, it sounded like the noise made by kids trying to create a disturbance under the Brooklyn Bridge or the sound of drunk Yankees fans after a win as they stumbled out of the stadium, but to the gathered women, it meant things were getting underway. Pushing and shoving in order to get closer to the bride, they all pushed their way en-masse out to the courtyard. Then out into the crowded alleyway where men in brightly colored outfits and shiny

Fez's were making the musical racket, and they all gathered around a sedan chair.

Aziza was pushed/shoved/guided into the sedan chair. It was a transport suited for a princess covered with white, gold, lace, and carvings. Torches—real torches made of wood and flame—were lit and carried by men on the outskirts of the crowd while others waved flashlights around the dark alleyways. There was seemingly no concern about waking any neighbors—quite the opposite. From the neighbors there was nothing but a vast enthusiasm as they spilled from the nearby houses and joined the wedding mob in the street. The women in Aziza's bridal party held their kaftans up high enough to avoid the donkey shit in the alleys and Colette was glad she hadn't yet put her spiky heels on as Aziza in her palanquin was lifted to shoulders by six of the most muscular assembled men and carried off into the alleyways of the night. Ahead and behind her the riotous musicians made sure to wake and notify everyone within hearing that something momentous was happening.

Several of the women took Colette in hand and dragged her along with the core of the wedding party making certain that she didn't get lost or left behind—as if that was possible with the noise and the crowd. The men carrying the sedan chair would, upon reaching a square or a slightly more open space perform a small dance while holding the bride aloft. Aziza did a good job of not looking like she was holding on for dear life as the men did their energetic performances with her held above them.

After a walk—and dance, more of a parade actually—of about fifteen minutes that seemed to circle around and around the Fez medina in tight circles, but that offered nothing that Colette could conclusively say she had seen before, the parade stopped in front of another set of the massive wooden doors attached to a high-walled house. This time, the massive doors were thrown open, and the entire procession entered an even bigger courtyard filled with men in fancy white and yellow djellabas—for some reason, Colette was most struck by the bright yellow slippers on the feet of every man in the room. They stood in stark contrast to the white djellabas and colorful kaftans that everyone wore. After a moment, she spotted Simo sitting with two older, more serious looking men. He was cleaned up and while he still had the pudgy baby face, she had to admit, he did look handsome in his wedding best—though the tall dark man sitting with him was more of her fairy-tale prince type. She guessed that he was the man Jamila and Aziza had struggled over.

The center of the courtyard was filled with another massive fountain, but this time there was also a wide-open space instead of a garden as had filled the other house. The sedan bearers and musicians moved into this space and began a death-defying performance where the sedan was tossed about and twirled all while Aziza continued to look regal—which wasn't easy

115

because it was her death they were defying—not their own. Still, the performance was astounding, and Colette had never seen anything like it in her life.

The fairy-tale prince watched with an amused smile on his face, and Colette was all the more certain that he was actually the groom in this wedding. With him was his brother Simo who seemed to have inherited all the baby fat in the family and a taller, gaunter man whom Colette could see as a combination of Adil and Simo. He wore a funny Abe Lincoln beard and with his features, it was hard for her not to start thinking of him as Honest Abe, though the Moroccans in the room had probably never considered it. There was a kindness to his eyes as he watched everything that struck Colette as being profoundly real. Certainly, he wasn't the most handsome of the three brothers, but there was something about him.

Colette caught herself—what in the world was she doing? She hadn't even been in Morocco for 24 hours and already she was looking at men as potential lovers. It was the wedding and the enforced separation of the men and women that had done it. She shook herself out of it and watched the performance and the three brothers with interest to see what their part would be.

Finally, the sedan chair was lowered, and Honest Abe stepped up to open the curtains. Perhaps he was performing some role as giving away the bride. He opened the curtains as the women around the room began ululating and chanting some sort of a song which sounded to Colette like "Ah, sa sei luda, ilay, ahmohmaadan ilay do dah! Lalalalaalala!" She was certain she had the words wrong, but she joined in anyway as they repeated it and ululated non-stop. She was in a different world—but the tune was catchy.

Honest Abe put out his hand and Aziza stepped from the sedan chair. She looked grateful and managed to look queenlike even though she must have been shaken from having been tossed around so much. As she stepped out, she looked up into the eyes of Honest Abe, and he looked down into hers. Behind them, Jamila looked ready to explode—Colette realized she had made a mistake. He wasn't Honest Abe the brother, he was Honest Adil, the groom! Despite herself, she felt a small sense of disappointment and loss before she realized the fairy-tale prince brother was not the groom.

The couple was obviously in love and the crowd pushed in close, the women trying to touch the two as if getting mojo from rock stars—Colette wondered if there was some 'baraka' attached to a marriage. The couple was guided to a pair of thrones that sat up a flight of stairs on a balcony and looked down on the courtyard below. Colette kept waiting for some sort of ceremony, but it never came. The couple went to the thrones and sat while everyone else began to dance, sing, and mingle.

At some point, young girls came through with trays of intricate little cookies and gift baskets, and then boys came through pouring tea. There was lots of dancing but no dance for Aziza and Honest Adil, no ceremony with solemn words, and no moment when someone said, "You may now kiss the bride, I pronounce you man and wife." Just the couple, sitting like royalty in state, holding hands as they sat on their thrones and sometimes whispering to each other or sharing a joke.

She was happy for her new friend Aziza and her husband Honest Adil. Even though she tried, she couldn't help looking for the fairy-tale prince, but he appeared to have left the wedding— which despite herself, Colette found a bit disappointing.

Your Chariot Awaits

Chapter 11: Your Chariot Awaits

During most of the night Adil and Aziza sat in state while everyone else danced, laughed, and chatted. Nearly everyone there made the pilgrimage up to the newlywed couple for photos like they were celebrities or wax statues. It was beautiful. Colette found the temporary 'celebrity' of the couple to be far in excess of anything that happened at weddings in the West. On their wedding day, Moroccans became royalty.

Over the course of the night, she was able to meet and talk with Simo several times. He told her that they would head up to Sefrou in the morning when daylight finally came. Despite her desire to meet Simo's other handsome older brother, she didn't ask where he had gone even as she felt disappointment at not having the chance to meet him.

Eventually, her curiosity could no longer be contained. "Was that your other brother that was with you and Adil?"

"Who?" Simo had his attention split in many directions. He was smiling at the girls, taking care of Colette, and chatting with friends. He either didn't hear her or had no idea who she was talking about—or just wanted to painfully drag it out of her. She refused to play.

"Oh, never mind. What time will we be heading to Sefrou? Are we sleeping here?" And so the conversation went.

The festivities went on until daylight crept into the courtyard. Guests had either wandered home or were rolled up in blankets on the floor, on the sofas, or against walls. As the party died down, Simo found her again.

"You'll probably want to change back into your own clothes before we head to your riad," Simo told her.

It was only then she realized that she had left them back at the other house where the women had prepared for the party.

"Oh drat, I left them way back at the other house where the women were. Do you know how to get back there? Can you take me there?"

Simo laughed, "Come this way please." He took her out of the big doors and around a simple turn in the alleyway, and they were faced with another set of big doors that looked suspiciously like the first house they had visited.

"No way, Simo. It was dark, but I know we came further than this to get here. It took us twenty minutes at least."

Simo shrugged with a smile. "Sometimes Moroccans like to take the long way. Aziza's family owns both houses, but they wanted to make sure everyone knew the party was happening. It's all about status and show with Moroccans."

He knocked on the big door and a sleepy-eyed woman Colette recognized from earlier opened it. She stumbled back to the changing room with the two following her. Women were sprawled on sofas and the floor—some of them still in their party dresses. Colette had thought they went home as the party dispersed, but apparently many of them had simply come back here to sleep when exhaustion finally struck them. She found her things and closed the door leaving Simo in the courtyard while she changed.

Back in her own clothes, she felt like a different person. Morocco doesn't waste any time changing you.

"Alright, let's take you home," Simo said, jangling his car keys.

"Don't we need to say goodbye?" she asked, thinking of Aziza and Adil and all the people she had met during the course of the evening.

Simo looked confused. "You want to wake everyone up? Don't worry, we'll see them all again. Now it's time to get you home."

Colette pictured home. New York and her little apartment. Nope, not time to go home yet. She still had a lot to do.

"Simo, what do you call houses like this?" It was so beautiful. She figured it was called a villa or a mansion, or some variant in Arabic.

"This is a riad. It's like a small version of yours." He seemed, once again, surprised at how stupid she was. She could feel it as he looked at her. Actually, that wasn't fair. He wasn't looking at her like she was stupid, that sounded too negative—naïve or uneducated.

"I have a house like this?" She was the one who was surprised. Her mother may have been right after all. She'd bought a palace.

"Actually, yours isn't quite like this. I mean, this one is totally restored and yours is much, much bigger." As she looked at the big garden courtyard, the three floors of rooms, the giant doors, and the fountain, she found it hard to believe that for what she had paid, she had gotten something larger than this. Of course, it was most certainly a wreck. A cosmic joke that the universe was playing on her.

They reached the car and Simo, who had obviously spent enough time around Westerners to understand ridiculous jokes pointed to the little guardian sleeping in the back seat of the Mercedes.

"Madam, your chariot awaits." She laughed as he moved towards the car. "Now let's see if I can get the guardian out of it. Sometimes guardians are the deepest sleepers."

Colette felt herself pulled in two directions at once. She was tired and wanted to sleep, but at the same time she was excited and had many questions for Simo. He didn't seem like he was suffering the least bit from staying up all night. Maybe he'd snuck away and had a nap.

The guardian woke easily. Simo gave him a few more coins and held the door open for her. Once she was in, he closed the door, walked around the back of the car and started the engine. Blissfully the radio was off. Yes, pulled in two directions. She wanted to stay and see more of Fez but wanted to see her riad in Sanhaja and that meant getting to Sefrou. She wanted to ask about Simo's other brother, but didn't want to sound like some desperate mid-life woman with a crush. She wanted to sleep, but she didn't want to miss out on the scenery.

"There's a blanket folded in the rear window if you want to lie down," Simo told her. It will only take us about a half hour to get to Sefrou though, so if I were you, I'd stay awake until we get you there." She was so exhausted. Jet lag, an all-night party. At least there hadn't been any alcohol. It was odd to see people enjoying themselves so vibrantly without the social lubricant involved—though she suspected that some of the younger guys had been sneaking out and drinking a bit—it was what all teenagers did, right?

"My brother thought you were very pretty," Simo told her. "He wanted to talk to you, but I told him to leave you alone. He had to go to work anyway."

Yes, she was so incredibly sleepy. "Your brother? Adil? He sat on the throne all night?"

"No, not Adil. My other brother, Yunis. He was sitting with us."

Ah, the handsome prince finally had a name. "Where does he work?" she asked. He was probably an undertaker if he had to go to work so early (or was it late) in the morning.

"He's the head of palace security," Simo said. "He does security work for the King."

"Really?" Colette was even more interested now.

Simo laughed. "No, not really. He's a baker, and he had to go and fire up the ovens."

She laughed at her own gullibility. Then, despite her desire to stay awake, she curled up with the blanket in the back seat and fell into a short but very deep sleep.

The Riad

Chapter 12: The Riad

Colette had always known that if you set your expectations low you were less likely to be disappointed, but somehow everything had conspired to create a sort of jubilant sense of what was coming. Even her dreams had her dancing on a mosaic floor and looking into a garden that bloomed with orchids and tropical flowers. She knew, at least the logical part of her did, that her riad, her house in Sanhaja, was probably a terrible little hovel. A wreck filled with rats and squatters—both kinds of squatters—the kind that moved into empty buildings and the kind that used empty buildings as impromptu toilets.

She'd tried to keep herself thinking grounded and thus, keeping herself from being disappointed when she finally saw her house, but she couldn't help picturing the beautiful Moroccan homes she'd been in the night before. She couldn't help letting the little girl in her have a fairy tale fantasy—just a bit of one anyway. And so, the inevitable happened.

Simo woke her up. "Miss Colette. Miss Colette." He was gently shaking her shoulder and gradually brought her out of some kind of dancing dream. She opened her eyes to the bright morning light streaming into the back of the Mercedes where Simo had opened the door. Behind him, she could see a red rock cliff rising skyward with mud houses propped on its side.

"Is this Sefrou?" she asked.

Simo laughed. "No Miss, you slept through Sefrou. We are in Sanhaja."

She no longer felt like she was in Morocco but instead like she was looking at some cliffside Anasazi village in New Mexico. A line of trees stood between the base of the cliffs and where they were parked. That, plus the sound of water flowing, told her that there was a stream of considerable size nearby. So far so good.

Still sitting in the car, she gave a little stretch and then stepped out. On the other side of the road, she saw a vast complex of broken-down buildings. Roofs had fallen in, graffiti had been sprayed along the walls, the once beautiful gardens that surrounded it were gone to seed with tree stumps that had been hacked apart with machetes. The disappointment hit her with an uppercut even harder than Destiny's. She'd bought a wreck.

"It used to be pretty nice," Simo offered hopefully. "I think with a little work, you could bring it back, Miss Colette."

"So, this is the riad of my dreams—" she murmured. Maybe she should just go back to New York.

Simo looked at her with a quizzical tilt of his head. He looked like a puzzled fat chicken from a Warner Brothers cartoon. "That's not the Riad, Miss Colette."

"But you said it was mine."

"It is."

"So, it is the riad." She didn't want to play word games right now. She was completely and totally devastated.

"No. That's not the riad, that's the hotel. The riad is behind it." The hotel? No one had told her anything about a hotel. Her riad was behind this broken down and ruined hotel. She felt a tiny tendril of hope spring back to life but quickly stomped on it to avoid repeating the same pain she had just dispelled.

"Who owns the hotel?" She asked, wondering who her neighbors might be.

Simo still looked like a puzzled chicken. "They didn't tell you?"

"Tell me what, Simo? Stop playing games with me."

"The hotel is yours too. You own the riad, the hotel, and about four hectares of land that surrounds it. This is all yours. It goes almost up to the base of the cascade." Colette hadn't thought she could be shocked out of her disappointment. She was wrong. She was a landowner? She owned a hotel? A cascade? It took her a moment to remember what a cascade was. At first, she thought of a mountain because of the Cascade Range back in the USA, but then she realized that in French it referred to a waterfall.

That little flame of hope flared back up; it wouldn't go away no matter how hard she tried. She would have to deal with it. She was sure that more disappointment awaited.

"Well, I guess we better go see the riad." She grabbed the big ring of keys that had gotten her into this mess and suddenly understood why there were so many keys on the ring. She had bought more than just the keys to the riad. She had also bought the keys to the hotel.

Simo grabbed her bag and led her around the back side of the hotel's ruins. She thought about telling him to leave the bag since she would probably need to find someplace else to stay, but then decided to let him carry it. When they stepped around the corner, she saw a big stone building with plain sandstone walls in front of her. Along one side of it a tin roofed shanty had been built. A few blankets and some clothes hung on a line beside the shanty.

The sandstone building had the same kind of big doors she had seen the night before and no windows on the lower level. The 2nd and 3rd floors had numerous small windows in it and then there were crenulated ramparts which stood above the 3rd floor on the roof. It looked like a fortress. The riad and attached shanty sat in the midst of a big garden that seemed to be well tended. The hotel stretched around three sides. Behind it was a steep slope that the riad seemed to extend into and out of. From this side, the hotel didn't look as bad as it had from the front.

The door to the shanty opened and an old man in a bright yellow t-shirt that said 'Brasil' came out into the light. His gray hair framed an incredibly wrinkled face and his toothless smile exuded warmth and happiness. He wore wire rimmed spectacles and a pair of what had once been brightly colored pajama bottoms.

"Merry Christmas," he said happily in very heavily accented English. "Salaam a leycum. Marhaban, marhaban. Merry Christmas." And at that point he and Simo were hugging and kissing each other on the cheeks. After a few minutes of Arabic chattering and greeting, Simo introduced the old man.

"Colette, this is Ahmed. He's been the guardian here for his entire life. His family used to work for the owners. He doesn't speak any English." He then introduced 'Miss Colette' to Ahmed.

Ahmed held out his arms and before she could say or do anything, the old man was hugging her. "Merry Christmas," he said again, oblivious to the fact that it was May.

"Is that the only English he knows?" Colette asked from behind the embrace Ahmed was still giving her.

"I think so," Simo said and then asked the old man in Arabic.

"H1N1, bird flu…. Merry Christmas Dude," Ahmed said happily. There was no doubt that Ahmed would be staying, Colette was instantly charmed by his warmth. She gently disengaged from him and walked to the big doors of the riad. Ahmed was on one side, Simo on the other. The old guardian pointed to the largest of the keys and then to the giant lock in the door.

Colette put the largest key in the largest lock she had ever seen. She turned it and heard heavy squeaking and finally a loud click as the tumblers turned into place.

"What in the world have I gotten myself into?" she said out loud as she pushed open the door of her new home.

The Strength

Chapter 13: The Strength

One thing for sure, it was going to take all the strength she could muster to make things work here. As she pushed the doors open, she was relieved to see that the house was actually in pretty decent condition, meaning that the floors, fixtures, and ceilings hadn't all been cracked or vandalized. It seemed that Ahmed was a vigilant guardian because when she walked into the courtyard, she could see a beautiful fountain still intact.

Ahmed grabbed her by the back of the bicep and directed her towards the rooms on one side. He reached for the keys which she still held and found one of the medium-sized ones. Medium being about seven inches long, made of highly polished and ornamented brass. Most of the keys had never really been gold, though Colette liked to think of them as such.

Apparently, Ahmed knew exactly the key he wanted because it slid into the big keyhole and turned easily. As the door opened, a rat scurried out and across Colette's foot. She wasn't the type of woman who spent her time screaming and jumping when things scared her, but in this case, she jumped and let out a yip. That thing had run right across her foot.

It seemed that rat catching wasn't part of the guardian duties because Ahmed acted as if he hadn't even seen it. Maybe that was the actual case, because he gave no reaction whatsoever.

In any event, he grabbed an old kerosene lantern and lit it before motioning that Colette should follow him inside. The room was much like the one she had been in the night before when the women were getting prepared.

The 16-foot-high walls were done up halfway with beautiful tile work in big bursting geometric patterns. She recognized some Jewish design and motif work and above that was more of the beautifully carved plaster work. Beneath the thick layer of dust upon the floor was more tile which was mostly intact, though some of it had been broken in the doorway. The furniture had all been stacked in the corner. She could see rugs rolled up and old mattresses that were obviously rat infested. The room smelled of rat droppings. Still, it was beautiful, but it had no windows facing out, only two shuttered windows that faced into the courtyard.

Actually, that made sense at the same time it made Colette feel more comfortable. The oriental view of the world was inward while the occidental view tended to be outward. She laughed at her own ridiculous philosophizing. She would have to go through that furniture, but she suspected it was all going to have to be either repaired, restored, or thrown out—probably mostly the latter.

The next room was in about the same condition. The glass in the windows was all leaded stained glass, and as she walked through and looked at the house she now owned, she was continually astounded that it was hers. How had she bought this? For one thing, it really was massive. A huge courtyard with a field of a garden in it, the fountain, dry now, but obviously requiring a significant amount of water to run and these huge rooms and great halls were what they really were. Rooms sounded too—insignificant to describe these.

She was already thinking about how one of them would hold a long table and the other would have her library in it. Ha, her library. That was a project that would take some time to materialize. The bathroom, well, there was a bathtub, but the toilet was a Turkish style squat toilet, and she wasn't sure it would function, in any event, that would have to go. It wasn't going to work.

A big dusty mirror showed the reflection of a tall woman in long black boots and tan trousers. Her white blouse looked like she had slept in it, which she had, and the black jacket she carried completed the picture. She already looked like a classic colonialist with Simo and Ahmed trailing behind her. Was there ever going to be any way to integrate here? Was that even going to be possible? Already she was looking forward to inviting Aziza for some coffee and befriending the woman. She needed a female friend here. She was certain of that.

The stairs going up to the second level were uneven and steep. Many of the tiles had broken loose and some slipped from their position when she stepped on them. The house seemed fragile, but she reminded herself that it had been sitting unoccupied for over fifty years—so, in fact, it had held up very well.

With the unoccupied time in mind, she found it amazing what good condition everything actually was in.

The second floor was still in pretty good condition. The exposed wooden beams of cedar were as beautiful as when they had been laid and while there wasn't the same ornate tile and plaster work in these rooms as in those below, the dirty white walls were a bit of a relief from the color and pattern overload she had begun to feel overwhelmed with.

She would make one of the rooms on the second floor into her bedroom. Eventually. At the moment, the house wasn't suitable to live in. It would need a lot of work.

The top floor wasn't as well preserved as the first and second. A falling branch had punched a hole in the roof and many years of weather and exposure had done its work. There was a fair amount of rotten wood and the smell of mold in the top rooms on the left side of the house. They would need a lot of work.

The uppermost level was made up of what seemed to be utilitarian rooms used for the kitchen and the storage. There was nothing particularly striking about these rooms, but she could see some potential for them, nonetheless. Ahmed led her up the final flight of stairs and used another of the large keys to unlock a big iron grate that covered the top entrance to the house. Colette understood better now how he had managed to keep intruders and thieves out. There was no way in unless you had the keys, or you went in the front door. The isolation of the house had certainly helped by keeping it both out of sight and out of mind.

From the rooftop she could see the broken hotel stretching around the property. There was nothing short of a complete rebuild that would bring the hotel back to life. A big concrete pool now filled with dirt and rubbish occupied a fenced yard—something would have to be done about that too. And she would need to do something about the rats.

Beyond the hotel she could see the line of trees alongside the river. Following it with her eyes, she could see that it led to a massive waterfall that came down in three streams. It was much, much larger than she would have expected, and she still couldn't quite comprehend that it was hers. Cascade was a nice word for it. It poured down the red, tan, and brown rocks that had been worked smooth by thousands of years of hydraulic action.

Colette began the short walk up to the cascade with Ahmed and Simo following her. The trail was well worn and littered with rubbish. Without the trash, it would have been magnificent. She reached the cascade and found more that would need to be fixed.

A carefully planned tourist deck, now broken and completely falling apart had been built next to the falls and then through mudslides and neglect had been undermined by the water and finally had broken in half so that it looked like some relic from a long-lost concrete making civilization. Several young Moroccan couples stood on the platform, alternately holding hands, cuddling, and then breaking off nervously and looking around to see if anyone was watching. Older Moroccans stood or sat at various viewpoints around the cascade.

An older Moroccan man in a dusty gray suit stood nearby. He had a big camera that looked like it had been transported directly from the 1930s. The big tin flash cone attached to his camera sparkled in the sun. The man's suit, his bad haircut, and the camera together formed a picture of a bored reporter waiting for a scoop. Actually, he was hoping to take photos and sell them to the shy couples that were there on romantic trips and wanted a moment.

Colette felt completely overwhelmed. The hotel, the house, the odd people she had bought it from, the fact that she was here, and that now—she apparently had two servants. A driver and a caretaker.

"Ahmed, do you speak any English?"

"H1N1," he said cheerfully. "Merry Christmas Dude."

The Hermit of Sefrou

Chapter 14: The Hermit of Sefrou

It was only a few days after arriving that Colette dove into the work ahead of her with fierce determination. She was consumed by a passion that she wasn't sure she had ever felt before. The initial tasks were ones that she could handle by herself and so she didn't hesitate. Simo and Ahmed both rolled up their sleeves and worked beside her. Ahmed sometimes disappeared and then would re-appear carrying a silver tray with glasses of mint tea on it or bringing a big tajine - the cone shaped clay pots Moroccans often cooked in—and setting it on one of the big tables that they had moved to the courtyard while work commenced on the house.

The wood furniture was mostly surprisingly sound, a result of being built of cedar and thus remaining termite and bug free for all the years it had sat in storage. Anything that was stuffed or woven was pretty well ruined by the rats and the pests. She was able to salvage around a dozen rugs and several carpets, but not much else among the textiles. When Colette asked Simo where they should take the rubbish and refuse, he told her to pile it outside. She assumed a truck would come and get it eventually, or they would cart it to a landfill at a later time.

Instead, bringing a small mattress outside to throw into the pile, she found a bonfire alight and Simo and Ahmed chucking other rubbish on top of it. Simo had a pyromaniac look in his eye and was searching for anything he could find that he could throw on top of the now towering inferno. Colette stopped him from throwing about a dozen perfectly good pieces of furniture on top of the blaze.

Later, when the rubbish had been reduced to ashes, Simo suggested that he could hire a few women to help with the general cleaning of the riad. This seemed a good idea as Colette wanted to get things as tidy and ship shape as possible before beginning any of the serious construction. She had been staying in the very tired Sanhaja Hotel about a mile away, and she was anxious to get out of there. As rough as it was, her riad was better than the rundown guesthouse she was staying in. She couldn't move in with it being such a mess, however.

The next morning a small army of women descended on the riad with buckets and brooms. Most of them arrived in Mercedes taxis from Sefrou, but Simo had also hired a few locals in Sanhaja. She recognized some of the women from the wedding and was happy to see Simo's mother in charge of the cleaning brigades. She barked out orders like a drill sergeant. No, she was more like a general in a wartime situation as she planned assaults, led charges, and inspected fortifications.

The women had a tendency to gather in the morning sunlight of the courtyard and fall into chit-chat but Simo's mom, who the women called Lala, would come catch them slacking and then scold and chide them back to work. Despite her size, Lala

146

was a powerhouse of movement and seemed to be capable of prodigious feats of strength. At one point, Colette walked into a room and found Lala holding a huge table above her head while two of the girls swabbed the floor beneath with old rags.

The riad cleaned up nicely. Surprisingly so. The garden in the courtyard was still a complete and total mess and the third floor was something to think about later, but the first and second floors looked almost livable.

"Simo, I want to go into town and buy a bed and some furniture. Will you take me?" Simo was sitting at the big table in the courtyard and eating fish and lentils that the women had placed there. A small tea glass sat next to him along with the crumbly remains of a loaf of bread, called khobz . He swallowed the mouthful of food he was chewing on and washed it down with a sip of tea.

"I'd love to Miss Colette. There's really only one place to get a bed, and it's in Sefrou. When we come back, I'd like to take you to meet someone who knew the owners of this house. He's very old, and when he found out you were moving in, he wanted to speak with you."

"That would be fantastic, Simo. Does he speak English? Who is he?"

Simo's face held a strange edge of concern. "No, he doesn't speak English. Don't tell my mother that we are going to go visit him; she doesn't really like us to associate with him because of the magic. He's an old hermit that lives in one of the caves up near the abandoned military base. His name is Sidi Ali Brahim."

The trip to Sefrou was interesting. Colette couldn't believe that she hadn't yet taken the time to go explore this fascinating old city, but then she had been going non-stop every day since she had arrived two weeks earlier. In the central core, there was a walled medina with massive gates leading inward to the narrow alleyways and derbs which were more like twisty, roofless hallways. Outside the walls vegetable sellers and junk merchants hawked their wares. Many of them women who had come in from the surrounding hills to sell their family clothing, tools, or household goods so that they could buy food. She was astounded at just how many pairs of used shoes were for sale. As she looked at them, she noticed something funny.

"Simo, I see lots of shoes but only one of each one. Why is that?"

"It's for security, Miss Colette. Nobody is going to steal just one shoe." Looking at the shoes, Colette wondered who would steal even a pair of secondhand shoes.

The mattress shop was near the big gate. It wasn't actually a mattress shop but more of a homewares shop. Six or seven big mattresses, kid bicycles, oscillating fans, big plastic washing machines, large, framed mirrors with Islamic prayers on them, and framed pictures of Muslim kids praying with Mecca in the background. There were big rolls of plastic Chinese carpets and propane stoves along with various cooking bric-a-brac and all the other odds and ends a household might need.

She picked out the mattress she wanted and told Simo to purchase it for her.

"How much do you want to pay for it?" he asked her.

"Excuse me?"

"What's your last price?"

"I have no idea. How much is it?" She was still learning that nothing was easy in Morocco, not even going into a store and asking the price. There were no prices. Nothing was fixed, not even in a homewares shop.

The girl who minded the shop stood there waiting for Simo to tell her a price. Simo looked at Colette waiting for her to tell him her price. Colette looked at them both waiting for some idea of how much a mattress should cost. It was a Mexican standoff.

"Ask how much it is, Simo."

"If I do that, she will give me a crazy price because you're a rich foreigner."

"She doesn't know if I'm rich or not. How would she know that?"

"You're a foreigner, so you're rich. Plus, everyone knows that you bought the riad so you must be very rich."

"Everyone knows?" she hadn't expected to be famous in just a few days.

"Of course. How much do you want to pay?" It was a nice mattress. Colette had bought a mattress in New York the previous year that was comparable and paid about $2200 for it. She figured the prices would lower here, but then again, they might be higher. She really didn't know. It was confusing.

"Simo, is five-hundred dollars enough?" The girl smiled like the sun had just come out after a particularly long and gray winter.

Simo looked like she'd spit on him. "Are you crazy? You can't just say a huge amount like that. People understand English. You're going to make everyone think they can rob you with your eyes wide open." He turned to the girl and made a hurried explanation in Arabic before turning back to Colette.

"I told her that you have $500 to spend on everything including a stove, a washing machine, the mattress, fans, cushions, and other things. You have to be careful what you say in front of people, Miss Colette. Everyone understands the money in any language you speak." The girl looked noticeably disappointed.

"Simo, how much should I offer?" That seemed to be the best way to go forward.

"Why don't you start with five-hundred dirhams?" He turned to the girl who now looked like winter had returned and personally offended her mother. From that point forward there was much violent arguing between the two that finally ended with Simo grabbing her by the arm and saying "Let's go, this girl is crazy, she wants too much for it. She is stubborn like a donkey."

Colette stopped him. "But what about my mattress? How much does she want for it?"

Simo looked upset. "I offered her eight-hundred dirham as the last price, but she won't go any less than eight-hundred-and-fifty. She's trying to rob you because she knows you are rich." Colette did the mental calculation. Eight-hundred dirham was about $100. Eight-hundred-and-fifty was about $108. Simo was dragging her away and leaving her mattress behind over $8.

"Simo. Give her the price. I want that mattress." She wasn't about to leave without it. Simo was not happy and got into further argument with the girl before turning back to Colette and telling her "You are making a big mistake."

She handed eight-hundred-and-fifty dirham to the girl. She couldn't have been more than seventeen years old and the look of triumph on her face was more than reward enough for Colette. Simo, however, was sullen and angry. He didn't like losing a negotiation to a girl.

"Her father is going to bring it to the riad later. I made her include the delivery in the price. Let's go." Despite getting free delivery, Simo was still upset. It was only fifty dirham and he'd managed to get the delivery for it, which sounded like a good deal to Colette. She tried to dig deeper so that she could gain some understanding for his mood, but his answers were monosyllable, and he wouldn't look at her as they walked back towards the car.

As they drove up into the hills towards the abandoned military base, his grip on the wheel of the car was white knuckle tight. Colette realized she had a lot to learn about Morocco and Moroccans. She wondered if he would forgive her anytime soon— for that matter, she wondered what exactly he was so upset about. There must be more to it than what she was seeing.

The cave of Sidi Ali Brahim didn't have parking nearby. Simo parked the car at the top of the road near the monument, and they walked down a dirt sheep trail away from the kids and young couples who were sight-seeing at the tomb of the saint. The green hills were scattered with rich red patches of soil and big volcanic rocks that jutted up into the air like parts of a modern art display. As they wound down the hillside through scrubby pine trees, Colette noted strips of dyed rags tied to the trunks and branches of the trees. There were odd, whitewashed stacks of rocks in random places, and they also passed a massive pile of sun-bleached bones stacked against a misshapen rock.

After something like a mile of hiking, they came to a small house that looked just like all the other small houses of the area.

"We're here," Simo said.

"I thought you said he lives in a cave."

"He does. Look at the house, it's built around the mouth of the cave. It extends back into the hillside. What did you expect that he lived in an open cave like some sort of neanderthal? This isn't the stone age, Miss Colette. We are not the Flintstones."

As he said it, they were forced to move out of passing donkeys on the trail. They carried yellow-turbaned Berbers who gave neither smiles nor greetings. It was odd that they'd said nothing as she had become used to the constant religious oriented greetings of Moroccans in their daily life.

"Why didn't they say anything?" She asked him.

"They're Berbers," he explained without actually telling her anything. He was still sullen over the failed bargaining. She was certain he blamed her for it, but uncertain why it mattered since it was her money that had been spent.

"Ya, Sidi Ali Brahim!" Simo stood outside the door yelling the man's name. There was no answer. By the time he yelled the third time, Colette was so annoyed that she took things into her own hands. Why in the world was he simply screaming the man's name?

She walked up to the big metal door and banged on it. Like most of the doors and windows in the Middle Atlas region, it was painted a pale sea-foam green. At first Colette had assumed that it was the primer color of the doors, but over the past few days she'd seen that it was more of a traditional color. Simo had told her that it was the traditional color of the Middle-Atlas and everyone used it. He didn't know why.

"Colette, we should go." Simo wanted to leave without meeting the hermit. He seemed nervous now.

"But we haven't met him yet."

"Yes, but the Quran says that if you call three times and there is no answer you should leave," he explained. Just then the big metal door swung open and Colette was looking into what could have been the tanned face of the shriveled twin of Pierre-Antoine DeFou.

The Hermit's Story

Chapter 15: The Hermit's Story

"Bonjour. Come in, please, come in." The hermit spoke English. He spoke English very well with a cultured British accent that surprised both Colette and Simo.

"I never knew you spoke English," Simo said in a slightly suspicious tone.

"You never asked. If it makes you feel better, I never knew that you spoke it either, my boy." The hermit sounded jolly.

He ushered them both inside his house. Once inside, Colette felt an overwhelming sense of comfort. It was not what she had expected. She could see that the house did indeed extend back into the hillside, but once inside it was hard to tell since the entire interior was bricked in the same way. The cave portion lacked windows but had another door which presumably led into the cave proper. The hermit led them into a big salon to one side that was outfitted with rich carpets and fuzzy sheepskins along with lots of fluffy looking pillows.

Pillows and carpets were the only furniture. Big shelves filled with books lined the back wall. The books were of many shapes, sizes, and colors. Candles flickered from sconces embedded in the walls and between the light from the windows and the candles, there was no lingering darkness.

The hermit kicked off his slippers and indicated that Colette and Simo should do the same. He motioned for them to join him on piles of sheepskins and carpets then settled himself down in a cross-legged pose. His simple light cotton djellaba was made of vertical white and light blue stripes and looked comfortable as if it provided plenty of freedom of movement.

"My name is Abraham Conver. People hereabouts call me Sidi Ali Brahim, for the simple reason that the saint on the hillside's name was Sidi Ali, and I live near it and Alibrahim and Abraham aren't really that far apart. Over time, people build associations between unrelated things, and I've become associated with the saint so that some of the pilgrims who visit his shrine even come to visit me hoping for a little extra baraka. Perhaps you saw their knots and cloth on the trees when you hiked in?"

"I'm Colette Samson, Monsieur Conver. I've met your brother. Though he carries a different name." This was a stab in the dark, but Colette wasn't certain where to begin this conversation. Simo sat in a dark corner and said nothing, brooding. He seemed betrayed by learning the hermit spoke perfect English.

"Ah, yes. My brother the Frenchman. Well, we've all adapted to our situation in life, that's certain. I've become a Berber saint while my brother has become a French designer. Still, at the heart of it, we're still the same Jewish kids, born right here in

Morocco. You can take the Jew from Morocco, but you can't take Morocco from the Jew."

"You're Jewish?" Simo burst out; he couldn't seem to contain himself. "I thought all the Jews left."

"Yes, my boy. You are absolutely right. They all left. Some of them left by leaving and some of them left by becoming Muslim. I'm of the second variety. Allah alahi illahla wa Mohammadan ala rassullah."

"Hamdillah," Simo said. "A Jew who became Muslim. God really is great."

Abraham laughed. "The first Muslims were mostly Jews. In fact, I don't think there is as much difference between Jews and Muslims as you might expect but that could be a conversation for a different day. I'd appreciate it if you kept my heritage to yourself, just to keep things calm and peaceful. Some people have old and ugly ideas."

Simo looked as if he wanted to say something and stared at his feet. "I'm not going to lie to my mom," he muttered.

Abraham continued, "Of course, I understand if you feel like you need to say something to someone. Did you know that your grandfather and my father went to the same synagogue? In fact, your family and mine were quite close back in those days. My mother would visit your family home in the Mellah, and we would all celebrate the high holidays together at my family's home—but of course, your mother was only an infant then." He let his words trail off to give Simo time to connect the dots.

"You mean..." Simo began.

"Al hamdillilah," Abraham said. "God is truly great for converting yahoodie to Muslims, isn't he?" Simo swallowed and repeated the god-is-great phrase "al-Hamdillah."

"And that brings me to the matter at hand." Abraham turned to Colette. "My family home. I understand that you bought it from my brother. Did he tell you the history of it?"

Colette nodded; she was beginning to wonder if this was going to turn into some sort of big family property dispute. "They told me some. I know it was built by your ancestor, Nicholas Conver. I know that the walls are oriented in a certain way. I met your sister Chloe, and she explained..."

Abraham stood up. "That's not possible."

Colette remained sitting. "Obviously it is possible because she was the one who explained about the way the house is built, although she also told me about secret doors and things underneath that I haven't seen any sign of. Do you know about those?"

Abraham had walked to the shelves and pulled an ancient album from them. "It's not possible that you met with my sister. You are mistaken. Also, there's nothing under the house but dirt—no secret passages. Someone has had some fun with you."

"No," Colette said. "I'm not mistaken. She was very kind, and her jewelry was magnificent. In fact, I'd love to see her again."

"So would I," Abraham said, "But the fact that she's been dead since 1929 makes that pretty well impossible."

Colette's mind refused to accept what he was saying. She latched onto the obvious thing he'd just said which was obviously a lie. "That's impossible. If your sister died in 1929, that would mean that you and Pierre-Antoine would have to be well over a hundred-years-old. I've met your brother, and now I see you. Neither of you are anywhere near that old."

"Looks are often deceiving, and we are both far older than we look. I was born in 1911, Pierre-Antoine was born in 1916, our older sister Chloe was born in 1906 and died when she was twenty-three years old. So there really is no way that you met her. It must have been someone else and you are obviously mistaken." He was opening up the album, going through the pages as he spoke.

"Here is a picture of my entire family from 1928. We took a trip to Marseille and had this picture taken while we were there.

161

The little guy is Pierre-Antoine, that's me in the middle, and the pretty girl with the bobbed haircut is Chloe. She was so pretty. These are our parents on either side of us. It was such a fabulous time then, the whole world seemed to be waiting to fulfill our dreams..."

Colette stared at the picture. The girl in the picture was the woman who had given her the keys. There was no doubt about it. The woman had been about twenty years older than the girl in the picture, by looks anyway, but it was clearly her. Of course, even if Chloe had survived, she would have been more than 110-years old, and there was no way the woman in Monsieur DeFou's shop had been anywhere near that age. Forty, maybe, a well-preserved fifty, possibly, but over a hundred. Not remotely possible.

The realms of what was remotely possible seemed to be changing rapidly, however. She'd been given the keys to a magic house by a dead girl who had apparently gotten older after dying. There was no longer room for the unimaginable to be taken out of the equation. She stared at the picture but didn't bother to protest. It was weird enough being in Morocco and discovering herself while discovering a very foreign culture, but things just kept getting more strange as the days went by.

"I want to tell you my story," Abraham said as he sat back down on the cushions. "Simo, my boy, would you go into my kitchen and make us some tea?" Simo stood and moved in the direction Abraham indicated.

"The wheel of fortune never stops spinning. It brings fortune and sorrow and just when things look like they are heading up, the wheel can turn so that they head downwards instead. Such is life and such is the way of life. Do you mind if I share with you?"

"Please do," Colette still wondered if this was going to turn into some sort of property dispute but figured that she was best served by hearing what the old man had to say.

"My father was a goldsmith. He worked in Sanhaja and sold in Sefrou, just as his father before him had. He married a nice Jewish girl like his father before him had too. My parents had five children, only three of us survived until adulthood, which was normal for those times. We had lots of uncles and aunts who were always around us and seemingly thousands of cousins. So many that we couldn't count them. We three children, Pierre-Antoine, Chloe, and I were spoiled rotten and given everything we could want."

"In those days, families like ours would bring tutors from Europe for their children, and so we had two instructors, an English woman and a French man. We were taught engineering, mathematics, French, English, and of course we were taught about the Jewish faith by my father and our uncles. In the Jewish tradition, the men teach the children about the faith."

"Pierre-Antoine apprenticed with my father, and I apprenticed with an uncle, a doctor. Our sister wanted to study with my father as well, but in those days, it wasn't proper for a woman to work with metal. Instead, she was forced to learn garment making. It was expected that she would eventually be a homemaker and a mother. She hated that. She pressed Pierre-Antoine and I to teach her our lessons each night and so, in a way, she was also an apprentice to our father and uncle, but without them knowing it. "

"Our French tutor fell deeply in love with her. He begged her to run away with him to France. He was a handsome and charming man, but she wanted nothing to do with him. Instead, she had a secret love affair with our cook's son. He was a Muslim boy, and while it would have been fine, at least in those days, for him to marry a Jew, there was no way my family was going to allow Chloe to marry a Muslim."

"We all saw what happened to Jewish women who married Muslims. The children became Muslim, and the woman was separated and distanced from her own family and faith—it was like death stealing a child. Besides which, the cook was far below our social status. She was our servant, after all. It was an impossible love affair even if the boy was our friend."

"Our French teacher, however, was something else. He was cultivated and very civilized. He approached our father about marrying Chloe and there was much talk of what the dowry would be. Pierre-Antoine and I loved the idea because we adored him. We thought it would be wonderful to have our dashing instructor for a brother-in-law. The stories of his exploits in the First World War captivated us. He had been a pilot in the nascent French Air Corps. He'd flown with the 124th Escadrille and done reconnaissance along the German disputed territories. He was a hero to us, but Chloe couldn't be bothered about him, he bored her. Still, it was a good match in my father's eyes, and so we took the trip to Marseille in 1928 to meet with his family."

"Ahh," Colette suspected she was starting to understand what had happened to Chloe.

"It was wonderful for all of us and perhaps Chloe even began to warm up to her fate. The tutor, his name was Gerard, was a good and kind man. His family was well off. He'd become a tutor after the war because shrapnel had taken part of his vision and made it impossible for him to fly. His family didn't mind that we were Jews, which was a big concern in those days, and my father didn't mind that they were Christian as he'd had enough conversations with Gerard to know that the two men shared a sort of agnostic view of God. The children wouldn't be brought up to hate their heritage on either side, and that was the important part."

"The details of the arrangement were agreed upon, and so we returned to Sefrou to begin planning the wedding. Obviously, Chloe had to end things with the cook's son, and that didn't go so well as you shall soon see. The boy was heart-broken, and no one could do anything to console him. They found him floating in the quarry pond about a kilometer from here—which was owned by Simo's grandfather. It was presumed by most that he had been hiking on the cliffs above it and slipped to his death. No one said it, but we all knew it was more likely that he had killed himself over losing Chloe. Muslim's who kill themselves are excluded from heaven and instead sent to hell. No one wanted to admit what had really happened."

"Chloe was devastated by the death of her love but over time, she healed. She began to press me more intently about my studies with my uncle the doctor and oddly, but much to everyone's relief, she seemed to form an almost impossible bond with the cook. As for the cook, the death of her son was one of those things that happen in the life of poor Moroccans. She screamed and wailed and wore black for the rest of the time we knew her. Yet, she continued at her job after a short time off, and as I said, began to spend more and more time with Chloe who now seemed to have developed a deep fascination for cooking."

"We didn't know it at the time, but Chloe was sneaking into the Sefrou medina and working with the l'fkih, the black magician. She was learning about spells, magic, and the world of the djinn. As the wedding plans were made, on the surface everything seemed to be moving towards normalcy. Chloe even seemed to be developing feelings for Gerard and there were times when we would see her looking at him from across the room with lightly teared eyes and a tender heart. The death of the boy was terrible, but everyone recovered. Or so we thought."

"The wedding was beautiful. It was a huge affair attended by Christians, Muslims, and Jews at our house near the cascade. Your house near the cascade, I mean. I have some pictures in that album, if you'd like to see—"

Colette turned the pages and saw pictures of the young couple. Chloe was radiant and Gerard, the young airman, was indeed handsome and dashing. The bride wore a gorgeous kaftan. In fact, the wedding didn't look so different from the Moroccan Muslim wedding she'd seen upon arriving in Fez. The bride and groom were sitting in thrones, watching as the guests danced. Simo arrived back in the room with the tea.

He looked down at the pictures. "It's a Moroccan wedding," he said.

"Yes, that's exactly what it was," Abraham said. "A Moroccan wedding of a Jew and a Christian. This particular wedding did not have a fairy-tale ending, however. I don't know who decided to let the cook whose boy had killed himself, when he heard about the union, make and serve the food to the couple, but they were both dead within a matter of hours. The cook disappeared and was never seen again. It was said that she'd poisoned Chloe and Gerard in order to take revenge against them for the death of her son. It didn't matter why, only that they were both gone."

Colette felt tears in her eyes. It was a terrible story. She experienced an acute cognitive dissonance however, since she had memories of meeting Chloe, who had obviously not been dead despite the tragic events which had happened in her house. "It's awful," she said, wiping away a tear. "It happened in the riad?"

"Yes," Abraham said to her. "I'm sorry to tell you it did. There was much that happened in that house, both good and bad. For me, this was the worst. The loss of our sister and Gerard was devastating. This is the way the wheel of fortune turns though. They are both buried in the Jewish cemetery if you want to visit their graves, but there is more I need to tell you."

"I'm telling you these things, because as the owner of the house, you need to understand that everything connects. The world is composed of a wondrous design, and if you pay attention, you can begin to make sense of the patterns and cycles that it forms. The mysterious universal laws that we all know, deep within ourselves, exist but only if you stop trying to make sense of them."

"I've spent my life studying the arcane arts and trying to make sense of the divine. In my youth, I was a doctor, in my middle years when the Jews all began to leave Sefrou, I abandoned my practice, abandoned my family and friends, and came here to become a troglodyte, a cave dweller."

"Since that time, I've spent my time studying, writing and contemplating these things. My brother, my cousins, and other members of my family all chose to leave. Some of them went to Montreal in Canada, some to Paris and Marseille, some to Israel. None of them have come back and if they had, they wouldn't know that I am here. It's been hard to disappear, and it was harder to become something other than a crazy old Jewish hermit."

"The house of my family is now the house of your family. In that process, your past and future have become intertwined with our own. The story of Chloe and the fact that you thought you met her are not coincidence. The beauty and order of the world is hidden from us, but if you are seeking answers, you don't need to look further than what most people call coincidence."

"I urge you, Miss Samson, to carefully consider the story of Chloe and what she might be trying to tell you. There is a rare chance in all of this for you, a chance to come to the sort of understanding about the miraculous nature of destiny that most people are never rewarded with. You are heading rapidly towards some momentous turning point in your life. And I, of all people, should not have doubted you. I apologize because maybe you did meet her. After all, it wouldn't surprise me if that girl had figured some way to reach out from beyond the land of the dead to touch us all in the land of the living. She was that kind of determined person. She could do anything she set her mind to, much like yourself I am guessing."

Colette was pummeled by a chaos of emotion as she sat in the cave salon watching the candlelight flicker in the sconces and Moroccan lamps. The shadows on the walls moved like living things, and she felt goosebumps begin to erupt from her neck and downward. The heavy sadness that had filled her moments before was suddenly replaced by a feeling of urgent action. She needed to get back to the riad, she needed to get out of here.

Suddenly, she pictured herself as a tiny little speck on a giant chalkboard trying to avoid being crushed by the lines that were being drawn around her. She could readily believe as she sat there in the hermit's cave that her destiny was being drawn around her. It was absolutely terrifying but, at the same time, the terror restored a sense of purpose that had somehow been missing from her life for God knows how long. The wheel of fortune had brought her here. Perhaps there was some reason in all of it. It was her quest to discover that reason.

Spiritual Justice

Chapter 16: Spiritual Justice

Simo had been sulking about losing a bargaining match to a young girl, but eventually got over it. Colette was still impressed with the deal he'd gotten her, and when she mentioned that he returned to his usual cheerful pleasant self. The mattress was delivered and with the help of Lala and the girls, Colette set up her bedroom in the second-floor apartment. She'd managed to adjust to the situation of the Turkish toilet but resolved that she would have a beautiful western bathroom (or three) installed before any other major work was begun.

Lala's army of cleaning women arrived each day and dove into tasks that Colette would have never thought of. They brought huge buckets and washed all the old carpets and rugs then carried them to the roof where they hung them over the sides of the building to dry in the sunlight. They brought huge bags of green beans, lima beans, and bunches of turnips and women would sit in the courtyard, peeling, snapping, washing, sorting, and then they would move to the kitchen they'd put together in the room that was dug into the hillside.

Without her having said anything to anyone, workmen arrived and began to fix the tile work, which she learned was called zelij. Simo and Ahmed took the roles of foreman over this grand enterprise of restoration that was unfolding. The second-floor bedroom-apartment had come together nicely, and Colette decided it was time to finally move into her riad.

The entire property was still rough, and she hadn't found where even half the keys went, but she felt like she could be secure there. Frankly, staying in the hotel down the road had begun to feel somewhat oppressive. There was a hotel bar that was filled each night with the seediest of men, and she heard drunken conversations in slurred Arabic that she didn't want to know the meaning of Arguments broke out as the men became inebriated, and women of questionable morals danced and laughed in the most obnoxious drunken way. Colette would have been fine with all of that, if she hadn't had to hear the sounds of them moaning in the night as she tried to go to sleep. The hotel felt like she was staying in a brothel, and this made the idea of moving into a half-derelict house with no other inhabitants sound pretty good.

"Simo, I want you to go get my things from the hotel. I'm moving into the riad today." She'd had electricity turned on, Simo told her that he'd made the appointment for the telephone to be installed, but there was a three-month wait for internet. The women came each day to do the cooking, cleaning, washing, and visiting—she couldn't think of a place in Morocco that would feel more comfortable.

"Oh, you can't move in yet." He said it so matter of fact that she almost accepted it.

"What do you mean I can't? It's my house and I'm moving in today."

"No, you can't. My mom won't let you."

"It's not your mom's house, Simo, and why in the world would she care if I moved in here?"

Simo got that look again. She had come to recognize it as the look of when something that he thought was important but didn't want to say it out loud. It was the-he-knew-something-and-didn't-want-to-tell-her look.

"Simo. What's going on?"

He shifted on his feet and stared at the ground while mumbling a denial.

"Tell me or I'll tell your mom we went and visited the hermit." There was no way she was letting this go. She would blackmail it out of him if that was the only way. The fear of his mother might be the only thing that could overcome the fear of his mother. He looked up at her with hurt in his eyes, betrayed by her threatening. She could see that too. Those hurt puppy dog eyes and then a flash of anger before a sigh of resignation.

"Okay, fine. If you have to know, your house is haunted. It's why my mom brings all these women here. She wants the djinn to start to think that the house is filled with people, and they go away."

She knew it was going to be something like that. They were trying to protect her from ghosts. Even in such a short time, she had learned that Morocco might be the most superstitious country in the world. The more she was here, the more she realized that daily life was ruled by spirits, djinn, ghosts, and demons. People here made important, life-changing decisions based on things that no one could see. Colette had transitioned from a stark disbelief to an agnostic 'I don't know' and finally to sometimes thinking she saw things in the shadows that couldn't possibly be there. The complete belief of the people around her was having an effect on her. The country and the riad were having an effect on her.

"Simo, go get my things. I'm moving in today." It was an order from his employer, and the young man turned and left. As he was going out, she saw him stop to speak with his mother. Lala flew into a rage and erupted into action. She began yelling at Colette from across the yard, moving closer and waving her hands like a mad woman. Simo was behind her, not even trying to translate. Colette didn't need the translation anyway; she knew what the woman was saying. She wasn't about to be bullied. This was her house.

She stood with her hands on her hips, resolute. No one could take a beating like Colette, and no one was more stubborn. "Simo, go get my things. Tell your mother that I've made up my mind and that I'm not going to change it."

"Mama, mama," Simo was like a child, grabbing his mother's skirts and trying to turn her from where she was still madly moving forward. She finally turned and screamed at him before turning back to Colette and wagging her fingers in the universal sign of a disapproving mother. "Hsuma, bento. Hsuma, hsuma, hshumalik!"

She turned and began issuing orders like a general under assault. The women had gathered behind her to watch the conflict. Fielding her troops before a last-ditch defensive battle, Lala was in action. Simo slunk out the front gate to go get Colette's things. She'd given him enough money to pay workers and make sure each day's food was paid for. He would have enough to pay the bill. She hoped that he was keeping track of the money in the accounts book she'd given him. The first $1000 was a test. It came out to roughly 8800 dirhams, and she wondered how long it would last.

Over the next hour, on Lala's orders, women fetched packages, chickens, herbs, cloth, and other assortment oddities. There was a part of Colette that wanted to tell the woman to stop whatever it was that she was doing, but she held back through equal parts fascination and intimidation. The truth was, she had won, and if she wanted to make peace, she needed to let Lala have whatever victory she was salvaging.

The assembled packages, animals, and goods were laid out near the big empty fountain. Finally, Simo and Ahmed returned and carried her luggage up to her second-floor bedroom. Their return seemed to act as a signal that action was needed.

Lala gave a piercing battle shout, and all the women stopped what they were doing. They gathered around her, waiting for orders. With her left hand, she motioned for a young girl to open the front door. With her right, she sent two more women to open every door and window of the house. Like the conductor of a grand symphonic orchestra, she put people into action.

Ahmed and Simo were nowhere to be seen. This was secret woman business, and they wanted no part of it. They'd disappeared out the front door in the moments just prior to when the woman magic began.

Lala began to chant. Her voice was deep and powerful. Surahs, incantations, and prayers flowed from her lips putting all who heard under her spell. The hypnotic sound of her voice filled every space it touched, birds were hushed, and nothing but the state of trance she created seemed to exist.

"Bismillah, allah aalahi,

la yadurra, ma'a ismihi,

shai'un, fil ardi wa-l fis-samma'i

wa huwa as-Samai'u al Alim"

Goosebumps crawled up Colette's spine, down her arms, and around her neck. There was electricity in the air.

"La ilaha illa Allahu,

wahduhu la sharika lahu,

lahul, mulku wa lahul-hamdu, w

a huwa ala kulli shai'in qadir"

Grabbing a black chicken now, Lala carried it to the fountain holding it with both hands. She chanted louder with the power in her voice growing by the moment until the air felt like it would explode. The chicken had given up struggling, knowing now that it was pointless.

There was a moment's pause, a silence louder than screams. At that moment, Lala yanked on the chicken's head, decapitating it with the gesture. Spitting, she threw the head into the fountain while again chanting. She held the flailing body of the bird and allowed it to spout blood into the fountain like a garden hose. The blood spilled elsewhere in the courtyard garden and all over Lala.

Five older women now did the same thing with other chickens and sprayed blood on doors, drains, windows, and lintels. Younger women with bags of salt, spread it like grain seed in a freshly harrowed field.

Lala approached Colette and put the dead chicken in her hands. Any ideas of resistance Colette might have felt before were now gone as the shock of what she was seeing in her house hit her. This was black magic. The women were performing an exorcism ritual. Colette didn't know the meanings of the words they chanted, but she knew enough to know what they were intending. She caught frequent mentions of Allah and Mohammad that somehow made her more comfortable than she might have been. This was a religious ceremony.

Colette held the dead chicken in her hands, not sure what to do with it while Lala spoke more invocations over the corpse of the bird. Now she drew symbols and patterns on Colette's face with the blood soaking her hands. Taking the chicken back, she threw it into the fountain with its decapitated head. Lala then led Colette by the hand from room to room in the riad while chanting and saying prayers. The other women followed behind and echoed Lala's words in a sort of call and response.

Through the two salons downstairs, winding through the courtyard and the kitchen, a visit to the two toilets on the ground floor where each woman threw a handful of salt down the drain.

Then up the stairs into all the other rooms before finally going into the room Colette had chosen for her own. Lala barked an order and was brought a small dish of coagulating chicken blood. Colette assumed it was chicken blood, but really there was no way for her to know.

Lala drew symbols on the white walls of Colette's bedroom. Arabic words and strange symbols that looked like Greek or Hebrew writing. Still others were completely unrecognizable as letters but had the look of being pictograms. Colette had no time to consider them in detail as the procession continued on with more chanting and prayers. As much as she didn't like this, she was fascinated by it. Fascinated by being present and part of such a bizarre and grotesque ritual. The blood would have to go though, no way she was leaving that on her walls.

The same process continued on the third floor until they came to the room with the collapsed ceiling. In this room, Lala worked herself into a frenzy until her eyes rolled back in her head and she had to be supported by two of the younger women. Recovering, she violently began throwing debris out the door and down into the courtyard below. Rats scurried out in numbers Colette would not have believed if she hadn't seen it. They ran out the door and over the feet of anyone in their way before leaping off the balcony into the courtyard below. A pigeon which had apparently been hiding or nesting in one corner flew out through the open roof. Lala picked up a massive fallen cedar beam which should have been far too heavy for her to lift. Then she collapsed.

The women rushed to pull her up. Several older women continued chanting. One of them, a truly ancient crone of a woman, bent over like a radio antenna, grabbed Colette by the arm and pushed her to the stairs leading to the rooftop. Colette wanted to help Lala, but she also knew that the work they had begun must be completed. It was all that Lala would want. She somehow understood that a balance had been achieved and stopping now would destroy that.

Everything she had achieved since arriving in Morocco had not mattered. This moment felt different. She didn't feel any fear, it was gone. She was sure that Lala had not and would not die. She knew, deeply and without question, that the woman would be okay. She told herself that as she reached the roof and was met by two older women with black scarves and Berber tattoos on their faces. She had not seen them before. She knew that everything was going to be okay. She knew that a victory had been achieved.

Hanging by a Thread

Chapter 17: Hanging by a Thread

On the rooftop, Colette felt something lifted from her, a weight taken from her soul. Looking down she saw her property stretching around her and far in the distance, the pale green glow of olive groves surrounding the minarets of Sefrou pointing skyward. Things seemed to take forever in Morocco, and yet when they happened, they took place so quickly that it was hard to imagine there had been any change at all.

In terms of the project at hand, as she stood looking in awe at all that was around her, the air shimmered and the chanting of the women came to a close. There was a deep and profound silence that stretched across the valley below and filled up all of the empty spaces in Colette, in the riad, and in the surrounding landscape.

Then, the warbling roll of the call to prayer came from the closest of the minarets. Soon it was joined by another, then another, and then many more. The timing of the muezzin was off just enough to create that warble of voices—almost—but not quite in sync. It was a stereophonic sound as the faithful were reminded to leave what they were doing and come to prayer. Come to prayer, God is waiting. Come to prayer. What you are doing doesn't matter so much as God. Come to prayer.

It was a feature of life that Colette, as a foreigner and a non-Muslim would never get used to but that defined the existence of the people of Morocco. Being interrupted in whatever you were doing whether it was by the call to prayer, the entrance of a person into a room, seeing a relative on the street or in the market. Everything had to stop for the greetings, the customary questions, the going to wash, to pray, to eat, to give thanks. All of the activities of life were unimportant when compared to the need to say a proper hello to each other as God had commanded or to pay respect to almighty God.

As the last sounds of the call to prayer faded in the distance, Lala slowly climbed the stairs to join them on the roof. Several of the younger girls supported her and upon reaching the top, she let out the ululating cry that Colette had first heard at the wedding. It was a sound of female joy and victory. All the women soon joined in. Even though she wasn't sure of the words or meaning, Colette screamed the joyous cry with them. A chorus of female happiness sounding from the rooftop of her riad and spreading outward into the world.

For the first time, Colette knew in her bones that the riad was hers. She would have to give it a new name. She would need to take ownership in a way that so far she hadn't. To this point, she had always felt like an intruder and colonizer. In this moment, however, she knew that it was hers. The words of the hermit came back to her, and she knew that all of the hard work so far was only a beginning. Her history had become a part of this house; the house itself had become entwined in the history of herself.

The person she was, the person who had always been hiding beneath the surface of her public persona, that person was now free. She knew that from this moment forward, she could let this house and this country direct her in the ways that she would need to proceed without fear that she would lose herself in the process. Her growth so far in life had been one dimensional but now, a confidence and strength had been born within her. It gave her a new purpose. She felt a guiding spirit emerging from inside her, making itself known. The Moroccan women on the rooftop with her were smiling and grinning as they shouted to the heavens. She felt like they, too, knew what was happening within her. She saw them for the first time. These women. They shaped this country, they built these families, they controlled everything from what looked like a position of being controlled. Nothing could be less true. Suddenly, she knew and for the first time she felt herself as one with them.

A bridge had been crossed, a place of understanding between them and she had been established. By taking part in their magical work, by being a piece in the overall puzzle, she had begun to make sense to them as a powerful element of the universe. Before, she had been an alien from another planet that had crash landed among them and was masquerading as a human but now, they saw her, and she them. Her differences were no longer something that mattered. She was still a strange alien creature, but now she was a strange alien creature who was a part of the community whole.

Gradually, the men—who had vanished from the site—reappeared to re-establish the illusion that they were in control. The women wandered away back to their own families, their homes, and their other duties. The work of cleaning was complete for now.

The house became a more male oriented place with the proportion of men to women changing daily to favor the masculine energy needed to restore and repair it. Men were fixing the zellij, repairing the room on the third floor, and ripping apart areas on each floor to install Western toilets and showers. Colette was doted on by all of the men, but she found that if she wanted something done, it had to be passed through Simo or Ahmed. Simo began sleeping in the salon downstairs, an arrangement Colette suspected came from Lala. Ahmed continued to act as guardian and foreman while staying in his shanty.

Colette pressed the old man with questions about secret passages and underground chambers, but he swore that no such thing existed. She tried to visit the hermit, but Simo told her that he had gone to Sufi religious festivals in the cities of Meknes and Moulay Idriss Zerhoune. There was no way to find out when he would return.

She spent her time wandering the nearby hills, tapping the old mud brick walls to see if she could discover the secrets of her house, and pruning back and restoring order to her courtyard gardens. The profusion of trees and shrubs had turned what once was probably a well-manicured oasis into a messy tangle of madness.

One particular plant, a kind of bushy palm that had impossibly deep roots presented her with the biggest problem. When she asked what kind of plant it was, Simo and Ahmed gave her an Arabic name, translated it as 'palm plant' and then demonstrated that you could eat both the stems and the roots. The plant was quite sweet, but that didn't change the fact that she wanted it out of her garden. Also, she wanted the fountain restored to working order.

It was a beautiful three-tier fountain shaped like a western wedding cake with a broken clay pitcher at the top pouring water that spilled into the three pools, dropping into the main basin. Simo suggested she replace the broken top, but after some thought, she decided that she liked it broken.

The first step to restoring the fountain was to restore the gardens. Colette found herself frequently digging to get the stubborn palm-plants out of the courtyard. She was making good progress, but near the fountain there was a particularly deep-rooted palm resisting her every move. It was surrounded by large stones that the roots had enveloped so the process of uprooting it entailed digging around the stones, loosening them, and then pulling the roots out with the stones attached. After several days of this, she'd created a hole two feet deep that extended under the fountain. Did this thing ever end?

Leaning down to pull a larger than usual stone out, Colette lost her grip as the stone fell into a deeper cavity down below. The dirt around where the stone had been collapsed inwards and Colette fell, her foot catching on the root that she had been trying so hard to free up. Hanging there upside down, one foot around a root, hanging over a hole that was so filled with blackness that she was unable to fathom just how big it was, she realized she had found part of the secret of her still unnamed house.

"HELP!" she screamed, and the echoes told her that the room below her might well be as large as the courtyard above. A fall might break her neck. One foot, hanging there, she realized that she might well be standing in a mirror image of the courtyard above as well as hanging in a dark hole. The mystic nature of the past days and weeks had hollowed out the core of her disbelief. The rituals, the stories, all of it gathered below in the inky blackness of a deep, dark, well.

Sparkles of light and the fuzz of static air in the blackness below—she imagined a black fountain extending downwards surrounded by upside down plants and a dark mirror version of her house. For just a moment, she felt like she was standing upright in the mirror image of her house with dark workers working on dark walls and dark zelij. The light of the blackness faded as she felt hands grabbing her leg, and she was pulled out of the hole.

There was no way to rescue her gently. She used her hands to protect her head and face as workmen pulled her from the cavern she had discovered. The secrets of the house were revealing themselves to her. She knew it would be dangerous when she started, but she now knew that the danger was far more than she had expected. Each secret would require something from her, but the vision of that black house down below didn't go away.

The day was too far gone for any exploration of what she had discovered. By the time she had been rescued, bandaged, and given hot mint tea - the daylight had gone. Ahmed put sheets of plywood over the hole she had revealed.

She was shaken by the idea of the dark house under hers. Did the dark house contain a dark version of her? Had she released a djinn or opened up a portal to another world? The practical part of her mind shut that line of reasoning down. It was just a cavern. No house, no workers, no mirror image. But she could swear that she had also seen two doors in the cavern as they pulled her out. One in the West wall and one in the East. She knew that she had the keys.

Death

Chapter 18: Death

The exploration of the basement, which is what she decided to call it, was put off for a while because of an emergency that no one had expected. Aziza and Honest Adil were already getting a divorce. It turned out that Honest Adil wasn't so honest after all, and he had been sleeping with her sister Jamila both before and after the wedding. Aziza found out the hard way, she walked into her house after a friend had canceled a coffee date. She caught Jamila in the act. Neighbors heard the screaming and intervened before she could kill either or both of them.

It was a disaster on countless levels both emotionally and financially. Simo's family didn't want her to end the marriage. They were desperately trying to convince Aziza that what she had seen wasn't real, that it had been some apparition or possession, or that it was a test from God. Jamila and Adil were to blame—but not for the act. They were to blame for allowing the shaitan to trick them. Aziza was not a fool. She wanted nothing to do with her sister or her husband. She escaped to the only refuge she could think of the house of her new foreign friend Colette.

Simo would have told his mother the whereabouts of the girl, but Colette swore him to secrecy on pain of losing his job. Meanwhile, Jamila and Adil had run off together. They had left town, and no one knew where they had gone. Lala came to the house while Aziza hid in Colette's room and complained about the whole situation to Colette. Simo translated while Colette gave him hard looks to keep him from spilling the beans to his mom revealing everything he knew.

In an effort to make some sort of peace (which Colette couldn't begin to fathom happening when the cheating couple had run off together and the bride was in hiding) the mother of Aziza—a sophisticated Fassi woman named Fatima-Zahara, also came to Colette's to negotiate with Lala about the best way to annul the marriage and how to make sure the dowry was dealt with in a fair way. Since Adil had run off with Jamila, it was almost certain the dowry would remain with Aziza. Lala was trying to save the marriage, and in a sense, not have the dowry leave the family.

Adil had paid a hefty sum, borrowed from his parents, brothers, uncles, cousins, and friends—for the right to marry Aziza. The money had gone to Aziza, and she had put it in the hands of her mother. Normally, with an annulment, this would be returned to the groom's family, but since this had been an especially shameful end of a very short marriage—that had been consummated—Fatima-Zahara insisted that the bride price not be refunded. Adil couldn't have his cake and eat it too.

None of this would have particularly impacted Colette's exploration of the basement, except that she was now roommates with a constantly sobbing runaway bride who had lost her husband to her sister. It was awful. Colette took it upon herself to prevent Aziza from throwing herself off the balcony. It was her primary task. Colette counted her blessings on not becoming involved with Simo's other brother, since the whole family now struck her as slightly insane.

Colette learned a lot about Morocco and Moroccans in those days of hiding Aziza. Part of what she learned was that Moroccan girls who spoke English had an excellent command of words that American girls also used to describe cheating husbands and boyfriends. Aziza had one of the most foul mouths Colette had ever heard, but to be fair, the two people she was heaping her disrespect on certainly deserved it.

Colette wanted to get away from it all, but at the same time, she watched with a morbid fascination to see how Moroccan families would settle something that would have ended up in massive lawsuits back in New York.

Eventually, Adil and Jamila were located. They had run to the city of Mohammadia and were staying with Simo's cousin who, once they ran out of money, began complaining to his mother about the freeloaders in his salon. She called Lala as soon as she got found out, and the hiding couple was revealed.

Lala sent Simo in his car to bring them home. She also brought the aldul (the officiating officer of the marriage) from Fez along with the marriage paperwork and a lawyer. At the end of the whole affair, Lala paid an additional fee equal to half of the original bride-price to the aldul so that he would change the name of the bride from Aziza to Jamila. There was no additional bride price paid for Jamila. Since Moroccan paperwork moves in a slow French bureaucracy, the papers hadn't been filed yet.

Aziza kept the bride price and none was paid for Jamila. The happy (but poor) couple returned to Aziza's house and packed Aziza's things and sent them back to her mother's house. Aziza, now less emotional since she had never technically been married and was quite a bit wealthier, asked if she could stay in Colette's riad in return for acting as cook and housekeeper. Colette agreed, and Aziza revealed where she was to her mother (who Colette now suspected had known she was there all along.) Aziza moved into the room opposite Colette's and began cooking all the meals for the household.

Aziza's cooking was flavorful, but everything seemed to be cooked for people who had no teeth—pressure cooked to such an extreme that everything crumbled upon entering one's mouth. Ahmed and the other toothless workers were happy with this. It was a cooking style born of cooking for her father and uncles, whose teeth had been prematurely rotted by taking intensely sugary tea and cake for breakfast throughout their entire lives. Colette missed having food that crunched but was very happy to have a female friend in the house, especially one who spoke even better English than Simo, even if she did break down and sob from time to time.

As for Simo, he doted on Aziza and followed her around like a puppy. Aziza wanted nothing to do with him but gladly accepted his gifts of food, electronics, and clothing. Colette had expected that the baker brother, the Prince Charming one, would turn up at some point, but it didn't happen.

Colette found herself in a strange place—never before had she wanted bacon and crispy vegetables so badly—but she knew that was probably a substitute desire for her body wanting to get laid. All of the affair talk had ignited her sex drive. It was a desire that could not be easily satisfied in religious nor in secular Morocco.

Still, things were fine, somehow. With Aziza as her new housekeeper and cook, her household had grown to four. Ahmed was a sort of overseer and groundskeeper 'Merry Christmas and H1N1!' Simo was her personal assistant, and Aziza managed the food and cleaning. Now that Aziza was in the house, and the family drama was so tense, Lala, Simo's mother, stopped coming as much. The workmen continued restoring the third floor and installing the bathrooms, sort of. To Colette's eye it sometimes looked more like they came to work to take smoke breaks. Life moved on, however.

Much to her surprise, the Moroccans, even Aziza, moved on from the drama in about a month. That was all it took. At that time, Colette was finally going to explore the basement, but then, Aziza's mom died. What would have been a distant tragedy before was now a death in the family.

There were some complications to the death. Fatima-Zahara was holding Aziza's dowry money. She left everything she owned or possessed to Aziza in what seemed to be a hastily drawn up last will and testament. So, Aziza inherited the deed to the family home, a large sum of money, and the family history. Jamila got nothing. Aziza's brothers were each left a sum of money, but her mother had known they were deadbeats, and anything left to them would be squandered and sold off, so she left the house, the business, and most of the money to Aziza. Moroccans have a saying that a son is yours until he marries, but a daughter is yours forever.

Family history is usually a bit cloudy, but for Fatima-Zahara's family it was a very concrete thing. There was a book passed down from mother to favorite daughter for generations containing all the details of marriages, births, business, and death. As a newly instated (sort of) member of the family, Colette was a part of the funeral ceremonies and mourning.

It was all so different from the New York version. It might as well have been the customs and culture on another planet.

Aziza was still living in her house, but her uncle and her brothers lived in the family house, which usually would have been the property of the father except for a contract that had been laid out by Fatima-Zahira's mother long ago when they were married. Aziza was now the rightful owner, but of course she didn't want to kick them out—or return. The mourners came to Colette's riad to pay their respects and try to get in good with the new matron of one of the most important Fassi families.

The full impact of the family history didn't really come clear until one day when Aziza appeared at Colette's door holding a very old book in her hands.

"Hey, here's a weird coincidence you're never going to believe. My grandmother used to be the cook in this house. How strange is that? I knew I felt at home here, but I never knew that. It says in this book, which is a sort of matrilineal family history, that she took a job working for the Conver family in Sanhaja. She says some kind of rude things about them being Jews that never should have left the Mellah—no offense."

Colette was neither Jewish nor a Conver, so she wasn't offended. Nor was she surprised. She had learned that nothing happened in Morocco without a deeper reason.

Temperance

Chapter 19: Temperance

Colette had nightmares. In most of them Chloe, the dead Conver sister, was screaming at her. Weeping and accusing. Waving her hands violently in Colette's face and shouting "Hshuma!", the Moroccan word so often repeated and used to control the behavior of others: "Shame!" Dreams about deep dark pits that she had to go down. Dreams about love affairs that ended badly. Nightmares about betrayal, death, strength, tolerance, magic, and love. The nightmares often started pleasant but then would descend into chaos as if her entire mind was being lowered into an abyss. Prince Charming the Baker, Simo's brother Yunis sometimes appeared, but even then, when she thought she might be saved, the nightmares ended badly.

She needed to temper herself. Take it easy. She recognized the signs of culture shock. It was becoming harder to deal with though and with all the many challenges and odd adventures happening around her, she was crumbling under the pressure of it. All things should be taken in moderation, she told herself, but to be honest, she couldn't imagine how to reduce the powerful emotional impact this country was having on her. It was all good to say that a little moderation was a good thing, but when it came to an actual temperance of something as elusive and unexpected as a total sensory impact—she wasn't sure how to achieve that. Her solution was to sit with a big mug of hot chocolate and take some deep breaths. What she really wanted was a bottle of wine, but even though she'd found a bottle shop where alcohol could be purchased, she hadn't bought any. She had never been one to drink alone. Hot chocolate would have to do.

The chasm in the courtyard had been widened. She had forbidden anyone from venturing into it before her, which was a surprisingly easy order to enforce. Not a single Moroccan among them wanted to venture down into a pit filled with djinn. She thought she would need to post a guardian to keep everyone clear, but none of the Moroccans would venture into it; they didn't even like walking by it.

Simo's mother suggested (through Simo) that they fill it with rubble from the hotel. There was plenty of that around her house. Simo said his mother wanted to come and perform another exorcism because by opening the hole in the ground, she was certain the entire house was infested with Djinn—again. There was no way to get rid of rats with a hidden nest, would it be different with spirits? Probably not. She would eventually clear them all out, but only when there were no more hidden doors. Colette shook her head no. She didn't know what to do, but she was sure that another exorcism was the wrong answer.

Later while Simo and Ahmed were buying supplies in town, Colette brewed a batch of hot chocolate for herself and Aziza. The two sat, looking at the hole, drinking hot chocolate. It was just the two of them in the house at that moment, and it was then that Colette decided to satisfy her curiosity about several things.

"Aziza," she said "Every other person seems to be going out of their way to get away from this house. You, though, you've just inherited money and a house. You have choices and yet you continue to stay here. Why are you staying?"

Aziza sipped her chocolate.

These days, she filled Colette with a sense of awe. The days of emotional breakdown were long past. No longer was there any crying or weeping. No more hair pulling or chaos breakdowns. She was strong and exuded a confidence that calmed those around her. Aziza was composed, filled with purpose, and suddenly completely unflappable.

She stared at her mug (milk with chocolate was what the Moroccans translated it as or 'halib bil shoklat'). Finally, her thoughts composed, she looked up into Colette's eyes.

"I stay because I don't want to leave you alone in this house. Bad things would happen." She said it directly and matter of fact.

"Aziza, I'm glad you are here, but that's ridiculous. Simo is here most of the time. Ahmed and his dogs are just outside. There are workmen coming and going from here most of the time, and I think that maybe you need to move on with your life, not just stay here for me. I don't want you to stay here just for me."

"At night, you would be alone here if Simo were to go out for tea or went to a cafe to watch a football match. Ahmed is old, and he is outside. It's not safe for you to be here alone."

"What is there to hurt me here? It's an empty house. This house is perfectly safe, and if you're worried about the djinn like Lala, then you don't have to be. I'm not Moroccan, so they'll leave me alone." Colette didn't know if that was true or not, but then, she didn't really believe in djinn, did she? It was a deeply uncomfortable question to ask herself at this point because she didn't want to give herself an honest answer. That realization told her the house was affecting her more than she had known. Maybe Aziza was right.

"Why haven't you been down into the hole?" Aziza and everyone else called it 'the hole' instead of the more comfortable 'basement' that Colette had labeled it.

"Things have just been too busy."

"And what about the nightmares?"

Colette hadn't said anything about nightmares to anyone. "What nightmares?" She wasn't going to say anything now.

"Oh, come on, I can't be the only one having them. I know they are coming from that hole. My dreams have been terrifying ever since you opened that thing up."

"Aziza, you've been through a lot. Anyone would be having nightmares—" Colette felt terrible lying to her friend, but she wasn't about to admit to her nightmares. Aziza was right and Colette knew it. She was glad to have her staying because the hole—she mentally kicked herself—the basement was filling her head with dark thoughts. That was it. Her fears were driving her. The moment she recognized it, it drove her to make a decision.

"We're going down the hole, into the basement tomorrow." She didn't really have the right to force Aziza to come with her, but for some reason she included the woman in her plans anyway. They would go down, she would figure out which keys opened the doors, and they would see what lay on the other side. Hopefully they would not release anything evil.

Colette shivered. What lay on the other side! If she were going down there to explore the world of spirits, death, and the paranormal, she must be brave. She reminded herself that she was only opening some old doors and seeing what was in the rooms. It was probably old, rotten furniture and caved in tunnels. Nothing more. She would be lucky if she found a tin spoon down there. Maybe they were graves. Filled with bodies...

She stopped herself. Aziza was watching her with those big beautiful wide eyes, sometimes it felt like she was having her thoughts observed.

"Okay. We'll go tomorrow," Aziza said. There was no protest, no doubt, no argument, just agreement. Then she changed the subject.

"I've been reading more about my relative, the cook. Do you want to know what happened to her? She tells a lot about the house. She tells a lot about the family. I've been waiting until you were ready to share it. I can wait more if you want, but I really want to tell you."

"No, I'd love to know more. Especially before we go down there." Colette was glad to be talking about something else, but she knew they were still really talking about the same thing. Aziza dove into telling what she had learned from the family diary.

"My grandmother lived in the kasbah of Sefrou, it's one of the poorest areas of the medina even today, and back in that time it was where the second poorest people in the city lived. Actually, that's pretty much still true, even today."

"Where did the poorest live?"

"The Mellah. Jews in Sefrou and Fez were salt merchants. The area they lived in was typically known as where to get salt. In Arabic salt is 'milhah' so mellah is place where you get salt."

"The Jews were always the poorest?"

"No. Not always. After the French came into Morocco, they built new cities outside of the old cities. The ville nouvelle was built in the early 1900's. Before the French, the Jews had been forced to live in the mellah, and it was locked and gated each evening to keep them inside. No one was allowed in or out. Under the French, the Jews could move out so most of them left the medina and moved into the ville-nouvelle."

"But the Conver family lived in this house for generations before the French came."

"True, but they were rich and had power. Plus, Conver is not a Jewish name, so they weren't really considered people of salt. They were foreigners with money. Not poor salt people."

"Salt of the earth—," Colette mused.

"Huh?"

"Oh, nothing. Go on."

"So, the Jews moved out of the medina, and the houses they left were then occupied by the poorest people who came from the surrounding countryside looking for jobs in the city. The Mellah became a den of prostitution, drinking, gambling, and crime."

"But your grandmother wasn't from there."

"No, she was from the kasbah. The kasbah was the next step up. Poor, honest working people with good religious values. It was also, umm, where people went for magic. Religious magic. But anyway, let me go on—" Colette hadn't stopped her but the conversation had made a significant deviation.

"My grandmother took a job working for the Conver family. She came up from Sefrou, probably slept in the house during the week and went home one or two days a week to take care of her parents. I learned something about her that I'm a little ashamed of, I mean, it's sort of okay in the modern world, but it's nothing that I would share with anyone else. I'll tell you but please, don't tell anyone—"

Colette promised that she wouldn't.

"My grandmother had been working in the house in one capacity or another since she was a little girl. She doesn't go into great detail about it, but when she was very young, she had a love affair with the man who became the master of the house. She must have been a child really, maybe just thirteen or fourteen years old, but anyway, she got pregnant and had a child out of wedlock.

She writes that her family convinced everyone she had been married to a Berber man who died shortly after the wedding was consummated. They used the girls' absence from the house, and the poverty of the family as an excuse for why no one else had known."

"People believed that?"

"People believe what you tell them. Look at my sister's wedding. I've already heard people recollecting that they were there, even though what they are remembering was my wedding. No one wants to call someone else a liar, and the brain adjusts to what 'reality' offers up. We all mold the truth to our own purpose, and if one person starts shouting 'Liar!' then it's possible that soon everyone will be."

It helped explain a lot to Colette, the Moroccan concept of the truth was a more relative thing than that of truth in the west. Truth was neither fixed nor absolute in Morocco. The past was changeable by simply saying it was different. Fascinating.

The cook's son had actually been a Conver bastard. The implications of that fact landed on her like a ton of bricks.

"Your grandmother's son—your uncle—was a Conver bastard?" Colette felt harsh using the term, but Aziza didn't take it as hard as a native English speaker might, it was a word with a definition, and the definition fit her dead uncle.

"Yup. That's the thing that made me crazy. But he wasn't my uncle. That's where it gets really interesting."

Colette wondered if the girl knew yet about the suicide and the love affair with his half-sister. She wondered if a woman would actually write about those things, but then, if she was willing to write about an illicit affair and birthing a bastard from her employer, it was probably fair to guess that she would write about it all.

"Did she write about Chloe and the tutor; did she write about—the suicide?"

"Suicide? What are you talking about? Who committed suicide?"

"Your uncle. Ummm—your grandmother's son." Colette explained about the affair, about the suicide, and about the marriage and death of Chloe. Aziza listened with a puzzled look on her face. As Colette finished the summary of what she had learned from the hermit, she finally thought to ask, "If he wasn't your uncle, what was he?"

Aziza shook her head. "He was my father." Now Colette was confused. That didn't fit with the story she had been told.

"That's not possible." That wasn't possible on so many levels. If that were the case then the boy must have survived, plus

he must have been very old when he sired Aziza, plus, plus, plus—
" It's just not possible." Maybe she was making things up—maybe
her grief.

"No, you've got to listen to this." Aziza began to tell the
cook's story....

The Cook's Story

Chapter 20: The Cook's Story

The cook was the first one to find out that her son and Chloe were secretly falling in love. Since she was the only one (besides her immediate family) who knew about the boy's true origins, she knew that the love affair was impossible. She couldn't tell the boy that he was falling in love with his half-sister, but she told him that it had to end. He, of course, wouldn't listen.

It was she who put love potions in the French tutor's soup, and it was she who told Chloe stories of romance and adventure that included a dashing young pilot. Using herbs, lizard skin, and other magic confections, she led the dashing young Gerard to fall in love with the young woman and hoped to make her son forget about his incestuous desire for the girl.

This, it turned out, was impossible. Finally, the cook had no choice but to tell the boy that he was in love with his sister. It was one thing to fall in love with a Jewish girl, but it was another to fall in love with your own sister. God would let a Muslim marry a Jew, but no man could marry his sister. The boy had no choice but to give up on the affair. He tried to kill himself by throwing himself from the cliffs at the quarry but was saved by a wandering Berber who swam out, pulled the boy to shore from where he floated unconscious in the quarry lake, and revived him.

It was the opportunity the cook had been looking for. She had been looking for a way to truly end the affair. Using her herbal powers and secret magic potions, she put the boy into a state of suspended animation—a sort of coma—and convinced the world that he had died. She hid him in the lower chambers of the house she worked in.

The cook's plan was to help Chloe channel her grief into a love for Gerard. Once the wedding was complete, she would take her son and start a new life somewhere else. It was a good plan, except that the boy managed to wake up, sneak out, and left a letter for Chloe, telling her that he was alive and still loved her. The cook caught him and made sure that he didn't repeat it, but the girl took the letter as a sign that there was life after death. Little did she know that her half-brother/love was being held captive down in the basement by his mother. For months the boy was held captive in the basement while the cook continued to work her magic on the couple above. For all the world, she was a woman in mourning for her lost son. In truth, she was suffering more by having to keep her child locked up and sedated.

Meanwhile, the girl took her letter from the other side as proof that life existed after death. She became obsessed with dark magic and began pressing the cook with questions about magic until finally, having no choice, the cook introduced her to an l'fkha in the Kasbah. Chloe was sure that she could find a way to see her lost love again, but all of her efforts to visit the dead boy were in vain because the boy was actually alive and being kept prisoner in the very house she lived in.

Finally, the wedding day came. The tragic events of that day played out with the bride and groom being poisoned. The world was sure the cook had taken her revenge on the happy couple for the death of her son. The cook was intelligent, and she also realized that even with her son alive, there was no way that she could expect not to be blamed for the deaths of Chloe and Gerard. So, taking her son from the prison she'd been keeping him in, she fled from Sefrou to begin a new life somewhere else as a new person.

The truth was it hadn't been the cook who had poisoned the couple at all. In fact, from the cook's point of view, it was obvious who had killed the couple. It had been Chloe, trying one last time to reach the lost love of her life. Or, possibly despairing of a marriage to anyone besides her dearly departed.

Hidden Doors

Chapter 21: Hidden Doors

"Wait a minute—you mean we're related?" Out of the whole story that was the thing that made Colette the most amazed, the fact that she was actually related to Aziza.

"Huh?" Aziza said. "Where did you get that?"

"Well, if your grandfather was a Conver, that means we're related. Right?" Colette was excited to realize that this woman she felt so close to was actually a relative, a kind of sister.

Aziza looked at her with a strange expression. "Are you a Conver?"

"Of course I am," she said, but then, she realized that in fact she wasn't at all. Why had she thought that? For a moment, she'd been so certain that she was a part of the Conver family, it was like their story had become hers by her moving into the house. She'd bought the house from them, and the house was hers, but as to the blood of the family, she was no relation.

That was odd, how was it that she had suddenly been so sure of the fact that she was one of the descendants of Nicholas Conver, the builder of the house. She'd thought she had taken possession of the house, but now it was quite apparent to her that the house had taken possession of her.

"No. I mean, of course I'm not. I don't know what got into me there, Aziza. No, I'm a Samson. This house is getting to me, that's all. I got excited about the story and somehow became a part of it. But it does mean that this house is part of your heritage. I can understand why you've stayed, now."

"That's right." Aziza nodded. "I want to understand more. I want to see the rooms."

"I'm not giving you my house!" Colette laughed.

"I don't want it! You can keep all my family djinn and ghosts. I just want to discover the stories." Aziza was laughing too.

"Tell me the rest of your grandmother's story," Colette said. "What happened to her when she ran away?"

"It's actually quite interesting," Aziza said. "I'm so happy that she wrote this history and kept this journal. She went to Marrakech where she was married to my grandfather. He was a wealthy merchant who owned several houses and trading inns, called caravansari. He made his fortune the old-fashioned way, by inheriting it and expanding it. Her love potions were truly powerful because despite having a son out of wedlock and being a penniless runaway, she managed to take a job with him and then to convince him to marry her."

"She was one of several wives and eventually, he set her up as the head of household in Fez. Apparently, in addition to being a great cook, my grandmother was also a very good-looking woman. She was his third wife, and everyone assumed that he had been keeping her and his son, my father, out of the way until his first wife had died. She was known to be rather fierce. People thought he had brought them down from the countryside and installed them in his house. I mean, we know the truth now, but that's what everyone thought. My grandfather always claimed my father as one of his oldest children."

"When he died, his fortune was split between his sixteen children. In some cases they sold everything and moved away, but my father inherited the house and business in Fez and became quite successful himself. He remained a bachelor until he was in his 60's. Apparently it was only my mother who was able to win his heart."

Aziza's eyes became glossy with tears as she thought of her mother.

"My mother was just thirteen when she married him. He was nearly seventy-five years old when I was born in 1981. I remember him, but not very well. He died when I was six. He was a very handsome man. Tall, strong. Beautiful dark eyes, and he could sing the saddest songs. I always felt like my father was my job to take care of—he went quickly though."

"He must have been an amazing man," Colette murmured.

"Yes," Aziza said. "I can't wait to see where my grandmother kept him prisoner. I wonder what it will be like."

She would soon find out. It was time to go into the hole the next day.

Colette suffered no nightmares that night, and the morning dawned bright and clear. Ahmed prepared tea and malawi, goat cheese stuffed pancakes covered in honey. Simo prepared for the expedition while the girls ate. It had become an expedition because of the time they had all spent staring at the open hole in the courtyard.

The gear was all laid out. There were flashlights, shovels, a hammer, a pair of big bolt cutters, a crowbar, and a shovel. Work gloves, buckets, and a hose that stretched down into the hole from a spigot on the fountain. The preparations were lavish for going into a basement, but such was the way of things when djinn were involved.

Fueled on tea and Moroccan pancakes, Colette was ready to go when another member suddenly joined the expedition.

Yunis. Her dark prince charming had finally appeared. He smiled and said hello in heavily accented English before diving into a serious sounding conversation with Aziza and Simo. He motioned to the hole and argued vehemently, and finally the three of them came to some sort of agreement.

"What was that about?" Colette asked.

"Oh, nothing," said Simo. "He's just my brother." Sometimes Colette had a desire to strangle Simo and his way of keeping things from her.

"He wants to come with us," Aziza said.

"Yes," Yunis said in velvety accented tones. "I want to come with you into the hole."

"H1N1," said Ahmed, the smile on his crinkly face making him look just like a skinny, tan, Santa Claus.

It was too big a conversation to have been condensed into only that, but Colette was learning that it was sometimes easier to pull teeth than to get complete information from Moroccans before they wanted to give it to you. Everything had a value.

As she looked at them, she wondered if Ahmed too carried Jewish blood in his veins. Simo and Yunis, were both descendants of Mellah Jews who had converted to Islam. Aziza, with the Conver blood coursing in her veins was also Jewish. She was the one who was an actual descendent of this place. Looking at Ahmed, she was pretty sure that he was exactly what he looked like and nothing else. Ahmed was a glorious old Berber with a huge heart and a handful of nonsense English.

Gearing up with the odd assortment of garden and hand tools Simo had laid out, they climbed down a wooden ladder that had been placed in the hole. Ahmed stayed on the surface ready to turn the hose on if they needed it. Colette had no idea what Simo intended to do with the hose.

She carried her big ring of keys clipped to her belt. The question was, did she want to go to the East door or the West door. It was a terrible dilemma. The lady or the tiger? She stood at the bottom of the ladder, paralyzed by her indecision, trying to remember the words of the woman who called herself Chloe— who could not have actually been Chloe. The house was oriented a certain way—which way should she go—what had the woman told her about directions.

Finally, realizing that everyone was waiting for her to move, she strode to one of the doors and began fumbling with the keys. It was the West door. It wasn't the first key she tried, nor the second. They say the third time's the charm—nope, not that one either. It was the ninth or tenth, to be honest she'd lost track. Meanwhile Simo was wandering through the pit dragging the hose behind him. Yunis and Aziza were having an easy conversation in Arabic. Finally, she managed to find the right key and having to use more muscle than she had expected, she turned it in the lock and heard the familiar sound of a loud click. She turned to tell the others...

That was when the explosion happened.

An explosion of water in her face. Apparently, Ahmed had turned on the water and since Simo had it pointing towards her, the water exploded outwards and into her face. If she'd had a weak heart, she would have died. The timing couldn't have been worse. She stumbled forward pushing the weight of her body into the door and fell as the door gave way. She fell into the darkness and heard the startled cries of Aziza and Yunis.

She was out of the water and into the murky musty mystic gray darkness of the first basement room.

The rest of her crew followed with flashlights blazing. Simo shouted for Ahmed to shut off the water and soon it stopped splashing on the floor where he had dropped it. The group of them followed Colette into the room and played with their lights on the walls and ceiling. Roughhewn, earthen walls lined with shelves filled with jars, pots, and ceramic ware. Two smaller doors stood to either side and the smell of water in ancient dust permeated everything. They'd found the pantry.

The jars and pots were filled with ancient foodstuffs and the ceramic crockery was empty, this was simply where it had been stored. The room was interesting, and Colette intended to call someone from a museum or something to see if there was any historical value to it, but there was nothing really extraordinary. No treasure or skeletons. It was like going into grandma's basement—which, essentially it was.

She found the keys to the two smaller doors. The first contained a small empty room. The other opened to a flight of stairs that climbed upwards. The steps were hewn from the earth and led to a blank wall that none of them was able to budge. She had found stairs that led nowhere.

Yunis and Aziza, bored, had already climbed up to the courtyard. Simo was still with her. He was excited.

"Colette, go up into the courtyard kitchen. I think this door leads there." Simo called out instructions, as she descended the hidden stairs to nowhere. "Take the hose and turn it on when you get to the kitchen. Spray it all over the floor. Maybe we can find where the water leaks out—"

Colette wondered why he had brought the hose down in the first place. She exited the basement pantry, climbed up the rungs of the wooden ladder, and felt an intense pang of jealousy as she saw Yunis and Aziza sitting together on a bench in the courtyard. They were having an intimate conversation. So much for her fantasies of a dark prince charming. God dammit. Why did he have to show up and ruin it for her?

She turned on the faucet and went into the ground floor kitchen.

"Simo!" She yelled. "Can you hear me? Simo?" She walked around the room banging on the walls and pouring water all over the tile floor. On the side where she thought the stairs led there was a big wall of zeillij. Intricate patterns with what she figured were steeped in Jewish and Moroccan symbolism. She was on the right path. She knew it, even with the pangs of jealousy she was now feeling, she felt excited. She was weeding out the imbalance she had suffered in the past. Things were getting better.

Then she saw it. A small stream of water running into the wall. She ran outside to shut off the tap and then came back to the wall, banging on it. "Simo!" She couldn't hear him at first, but gradually she became aware of a steady thumping to her left. Running her hands over the zellij, she found a loose tile and wriggled it. It fell, revealing a keyhole. It was a secret door!

Once again, she was searching through the ring of keys for the one that would fit. This time she got it on the first try. It was the smallest of the keys and when she turned it something amazing happened. A door hidden in the lines of zellij opened towards her. She pulled on it, felt a slight resistance, and then felt it give. As it opened, she could hear Simo cursing as he fell forward, then trying to rebalance himself, fell backwards down the steps.

It served him right for the hose in her face, she thought as she rushed down to make sure he was okay.

The Devil in the Details

Chapter 22: The Devil in the Details

Thankfully, he was fine. A big bump on his big head was all the damage he suffered. Colette helped him up and then strode purposefully towards the other door. She was tired of the secrets this house was keeping. She was tired of everything being held back and always being afraid that something else was coming. She was going to open this door and any doors she found inside. It was time to put the keys away. She was through not having all the information she wanted.

Everything was coming out now. She didn't care if Aziza and Yunis weren't there. It wasn't their business anyway and despite her DNA, it wasn't Aziza's house. Who did she think she was living rent free and taking any man that came into the house as if she were the owner of the world? If the cook had been like Aziza, it was no wonder she had been chased off.

Colette knew that her thoughts weren't fair, but she didn't care. Life wasn't fair, and she was tired of being nice and getting water in her face. She was tired of getting shoved around and bothered by people as she tried to learn and respect their culture, and they ignored hers. This was her house. She'd bought it. She'd paid for it. Not only with money, but with a bruised ego and now battered dreams where Prince Charming ran off with someone else.

Again, it took three keys before she found the one she needed. She was sure of what she would find in this room anyway. Nothing but junk and old dust. Rotting furniture and more rats—although, since the exorcism Lala had conducted, she hadn't seen a single rat or mouse in the place. She kicked the door open with Simo still coming across the basement towards her.

"Miss Colette, maybe you should be care..." he stopped as she spun towards him, then finished the word "...ful." He didn't know what had gotten into her or why she had that wild look in her eyes. It was him that had been knocked down the stairs, after all, but he decided that was all he was going to say. She looked at him for a moment, considering which limb to tear off first and then turned back to the room that had been locked since—well, since the family left the house.

Boxes. Wooden crates. Dust. Junk. She was sure. "Simo, get me a hammer and a pry bar." She walked into the room shining her light around to get an assessment of what was there. Some wood and plaster picture frames leaning against the wall with the pictures facing the other way. An iron bound chest was there. It looked like a treasure chest—haha. As if there would be treasure in a shitty old place like this. She felt the bitterness sapping away at any joy she might have found. Wooden boxes wrapped in decaying canvas. Despite her bitter cynicism, she had to admit, this was starting to look like a treasure vault.

She felt a sudden urge to shut the door and tell everyone that she'd found nothing. Aziza's new found relationship to the house seemed much more threatening. Colette knew gold, and she suddenly knew, without a doubt, that there was gold in this room. A lot of it. Had Simo figured that out yet? Was she just imagining things? No.

Aziza and Yunis were at the door now with Simo.

"What's in here?" Aziza asked. "Did you find anything?"

"Just more junk," Colette lied. "Let's call it a day. I can't breathe this dust any more." She turned and kept herself from shoving Aziza out of the way, just barely. Aziza was a man stealer, just like her sister, no doubt about it. No wonder poor Jamila hated her so much. Well, she wasn't going to get the chance to steal this treasure, that was for certain. Colette checked herself—it was Aziza who had her man stolen, her husband. And as for the treasure, there might not be anything there at all.

Simo and Yunis were silent as Colette closed and locked the door. Just so things wouldn't look too suspicious, she walked across the basement and locked the other door too. Then she began to climb the ladder up to the courtyard.

"You coming?" She said to the three watching her from below. The keys. She was the one with the keys and so whatever the keys revealed, she owned. At least she hoped so.

She knew she was being greedy and selfish. She knew that she was acting paranoid and kind of awful, but it was better than punching that bitch in the face and then kicking her ass. She reminded herself that she didn't know Yunis, but it didn't matter. Why in the world should he be interested in her anyway, he didn't know her. She didn't know him. He might be an awful person. Look what his brother had done, married the wrong sister, and then run away with the right one. She needed them to go. She needed time away from the house and away from Simo, Yunis, and Aziza, but now that she thought the house might be sitting on a treasure room, there was no way she could leave without seeing what was there.

"Aziza?" She said as the girl climbed out of the hole behind Simo but ahead of Yunis.

"Can you and Simo go get us some fresh fruit from the souq?" Colette couldn't help it, there was still a part of her that wanted Yunis, wanted to prove that she could make him want her. She knew if she could get him alone, she could win him over. It was the least important thing going on right now, but for some reason, her bruised ego had made it priority number one.

But all to no avail.

"Sure," Aziza said. "Come on guys." And with that, the queen left with her admirers. It was for the best, but still, Colette had wanted to have a chance, she wanted a shot at it. At him.

As the sound of the car faded into the distance, Colette got out her phone and dialed Destiny in New York. It was the first time she had called since she had left.

"Hello?" a sleepy voice said. It was early morning in New York even if it was almost noon in Morocco.

Hearing her girlfriend's voice, even if it was filled with annoyance at being woken from sleep, brought a feeling of homesickness over Colette. She felt tears coming. "Hi Destiny, it's Colette." She was going to blubber, no doubt about it.

"Damn girlfriend, it's about time you called. I thought maybe you found some beautiful Arab man and became a prisoner of lovemaking." Sometimes, Destiny knew just what to say, in this case it was just what to say to make Colette actually begin blubbering.

"I hate it, I hate it here, Destiny. I'm like a prisoner, nobody cares about me. I don't feel like I can go out, I feel like I have no one ...I ...I ...I..."

All the annoyance and sleep were gone from Destiny's voice. "Whoa! Whoa girl! Slow down. I'm here. I'm here. Tell Big Mama what the problem is."

Colette began to feel better almost immediately. She got control of herself as she told Destiny everything that had happened so far. Just getting it out made a huge difference— trapped in her own head, the whole thing with Yunis had taken on some sort of significance, but telling Destiny about it, she started to see it in a different light. Destiny was a great friend. She listened, and then she called bullshit.

"You have got to be kidding me, right?" Destiny said. "You're sitting there crying over a Moroccan baker that you've never even had a conversation with? Colette, get a hold of yourself girl. You might be imagining Prince Charming, but the reality is he's probably as dumb as a stick with the dick of a two-year-old. Hell, girl. For all you know, he's gay."

"And that girl? What the hell are you letting her stay in your house for? Did you invite her? Just cause her grandpa screwed the help don't make her the lady of the manor. You bought the house. It's yours. It's all yours. You got the contract with you, right? You got it all translated into English, right? Just read that thing and find out what's happening. Sounds like these people are eating you alive, woman."

"No, they're not. I mean, they're helping me with everything. They've done so much for me already—"

"Colette. You're paying for everything. Trust me. Nobody is doing anything for free. You pay your helper, right? You pay the guardian, right? All them women that came, you paid them didn't you?"

It was true. Simo had suggested it. He said that they had come, including Lala, just out of the goodness of their hearts, but that it would be a good thing to give them something. So she had told him to pay them what he thought was fair. They'd all been making more working for her than they would have been working for anyone else. Even Aziza, not that she needed any money, but she was eating Colette's food, staying in her house, and she hadn't offered to pay for anything yet. How in the world had she come to feel like they were all doing her favors? She had felt like she owed them, but actually, if anyone was owed anything—it was her.

"Destiny, what should I do?" Colette asked, finally. It wasn't like her, but she felt out of her depth. It had taken Destiny, the great manipulator, to point out that Colette was being manipulated. She hadn't seen it. Maybe Destiny could point her in the right direction.

Destiny laughed. "What the fuck do you think you should do? Go down there and see what's in them boxes, Girl. I'm dying to know if you just bought a big house full of treasure." Simple enough. But first she wanted to re-read the deed to her house and property.

After getting off the phone she went upstairs to go over the paperwork. It was straightforward and clear. She was the sole owner of the house, and all it contained. She owned the hotel, the land, and the property on the land. It was free and clear with no strange clauses or tricky wording. The one odd bit that she hadn't noticed before was about providing maintenance to any current tenants or residents of the house.

Since the house had been unoccupied, she hadn't thought much about it, she'd known there was a guardian and had figured the clause simply meant that she couldn't evict him and take away his job. She'd agreed to keep Ahmed on as a gardener and guardian. Now she wondered about Aziza. Did the girl moving in make her a resident? She was just a guest, right?

The devil was in the details. She was just going to have to ask Aziza to leave. She liked the girl, but she couldn't really keep her around anymore. It was too much strain. And she really didn't want to discover any treasure with a descendant of the Conver family living in the house. She felt a little bit guilty over that, a little selfish and greedy, but she knew it was the right way to go forward. She had to protect herself.

The Ivory Tower

Chapter 23: The Ivory Tower

"You want me to leave?" Aziza sounded shocked. "I thought we were friends?"

Colette attempted to explain things the way she had thought it out. "We are friends, but I'm having work done in the house and having you live here, makes it more complicated. You have a house, you have money, so it's not like I'm kicking you onto the street."

"But you are kicking me out." Aziza was both hurt and offended. "The white queen in her ivory tower doesn't want any of the locals cramping her style." It was closer to the truth than she knew. "This is about Yunis, isn't it. I'm Moroccan, I know when a woman likes a man. I could see it the way you looked at him. You didn't even have to say anything."

Well, that would have made things easier, if Collete were willing to admit it—which she wasn't. "I don't know what you are talking about."

"Oh, you know! Simo told me how much you like his brother. He's a little jealous, you know. Simo has a crush on you, and you've got a crush on his brother. And now, you're kicking me out because of it. I see how it is."

"Simo has a vivid imagination. Contrary to what you may think or what he may have told you, he is not my confidant, I don't run to him giggling every time an attractive man appears."

"Ah ha! I knew it!" Aziza declared. "You think Yunis is attractive."

Colette didn't believe for a second that Simo had a crush on her or that he had said anything to Aziza about her liking Yunis. It was clear that Simo had a crush on Aziza. This was just Aziza showing her family colors. That was what got her blood boiling. "I thought you said we were friends."

"Yeah, so did I, but now you're kicking me out." Aziza was making this much more ugly than it needed to be, but now that Colette had seen the ugliness, she was like an OCD bookkeeper following a discrepancy to the source.

"You thought I liked Yunis?" Even as she said it she felt like the 13-year-old girl she sounded like. She was admitting it, but she had to, in order to expose the crime.

"Of course I did. Anyone could see it? Especially a Moroccan. You can't hide things like that from a Moroccan. You are not a Moroccan so you can't hide anything from us." Aziza was putting Colette into her versus all of the Moroccans mentality.

"You thought I liked him, but you still went after him? Who's the real bitch here?" Colette felt more petty and more teenage by the second.

"Went after him? He came after me. Of course I let him, he's a very attractive man. It was his choice, not mine. I don't even like him."

"You still think you can say you were my friend after admitting that? After letting him think he could sniff up your tree?" It was a trap. Colette had opened it as if she held the keys, and Aziza had walked in and closed the door behind her. There's no country where a friend can go after a guy, she knows her girlfriend likes. No matter what your culture, if you did that, you were a bitch. If the guy your friend likes comes after you, you push him away. That's what friends did. Any other reaction revealed the truth. Aziza may have never heard the phrase 'sniffing up your tree' but she knew she was caught. It wasn't the Moroccan way though, to ever admit defeat.

"You're just making excuses to try to get me out of the picture now. You think if you send me back to Fez that maybe he'll come sniff up your stinky old tree. Don't count on it. He's hooked on me. That dog is mine."

Colette was surprised by this whole conversation. It wasn't the one she had practiced. Still, it was good. The truth was finding a way to the surface. Aziza was justifying Colette kicking her out more with every word she said. One thing was sure, she didn't mind sending the girl home now. She'd felt guilty before, like she was trying to rob her, but now, now she felt like she was reclaiming her house.

"Aziza. We're done with this conversation. Get your things out of my house. Simo will drive you back down to Fez, and you can have Yunis too. He's not my type. I'm not sure what you thought, but I'm not interested in players like him or in fake friends that don't respect me. This old tree has been sniffed at enough." It hurt to call herself old, but in a way, it was liberating. She turned and walked away and thought she heard Aziza mumble the word 'bitch' as she did so. That's right. She was a tough fucking bitch. It was time people around here started learning that. How had she forgotten?

"Simo," she shouted to the young man as he sat munching fruit with his brother in the salon. "Would you and Yunis please help Aziza get her things, and then take her back to her house in Fez. She won't be staying with us any longer. Also, I'd prefer if your family no longer came to visit."

"Miss Colette? Why?" He was confused and torn between keeping a pretty great job and defending his family. Maybe he really did have a crush on her. All of this was so stupid in the first place. Yunis wasn't any sort of prize. She'd built an aura around him, maybe she'd needed to have a light at the end of the tunnel.

Some reason why she had dragged herself across the Atlantic to a country where she couldn't even go sit in a wine bar with her girlfriends at the end of a workout. This whole thing was ridiculous. It was time to move on.

"I'm tired of always having people around. I want some me-time. In fact, I'd prefer it if you take a few days off and go visit your family. If you want to keep working for me, you can come back in a few days."

When Aziza and the two guys were finally gone, it was nearly 3 PM. Colette called Ahmed into the house and asked him to come down into the basement with her. She unlocked the door to the treasure room and had him shine the light while she opened the boxes and looked at the treasures. She felt like Howard Carter, the man who had discovered King Tut's tomb. A part of her wanted to keep it all a big secret, but she knew that was wrong— she needed someone else here. She needed a witness so that she would be compelled to do what was right—though Ahmed's loyalty was such that if she had chosen to murder people and bury them in her basement—he would have never told.

She knew that whatever she found here, she would have to share it—somehow. She was soon to discover that there was a lot to share.

The final key on her ring opened up the ironclad box. It was filled with gold coins just like the one that Monsieur DeFou had given to her. It was a fortune, and it was hers.

She became aware of Ahmed standing over her with the flashlight. She took a coin, and handed it up to him, half expecting the heavy flashlight to come down and crush her skull. Ahmed's three teeth were bared in an almost toothless grin as he took the coin from her extended hand.

"Merry Christmas."

A Star is Born

Chapter 24: A Star is Born

Moroccan Customs was a funny thing. It turned out that the biggest worry the customs agents had was that she might be taking 'precious fossils' out of the country. They asked her if she had any fossils, and when she said no, they didn't even look at her very heavy luggage.

She probably would have drawn some notice if she had checked a box of gold coins, a bunch of books written in Hebrew, and a huge collection of Jewish artifacts in rubber tubs. That wasn't how it worked. In New York, it was just a matter of paying the right people, right around $10,000, which, thanks to the machinations of Destiny, didn't have to even come out of her bank account.

The key was donating the Hebrew books and artifacts to the Jewish Museum in New York City. Colette agreed to donate the books, ceramics, and religious items of Moroccan Jewish origin to the museum in exchange for them paying the aforementioned $10,000 in 'transit fees' and transporting a few crates of 'personal items' that she didn't want to be bothered by customs with.

The iron bound box of gold coins, a couple of paintings, some beautiful ceramics, and a few old books in French and English were all delivered to her condo without her having to sign for anything at all. The Jewish Museum was exhilarated to have the items she donated and valued the collection (not including the things she had kept like the gold coins) at more than $15 million dollars. It was described in The New York Times as "The Moroccan Jewish Treasure Horde," and the museum named the wing they would be housed in as 'The Colette Samson Wing'. The whole thing had made her a star.

The whole process moved out of her hands with a single call from her friend Destiny. In a very short time, the museum's director had flown to Morocco to evaluate the potential of the collection himself. It never paid to underestimate the influence of a smoking hot African American model with a killer haymaker.

There were families who came out of the woodwork to make claims on the treasure after the announcement, both in Morocco and the USA, but thankfully, the announcement was not made until after everything had been transported. Families with legitimate claims received a cash settlement, added their names to the list of benefactors, and reminded them that their family's contribution had become a part of Jewish world heritage. The combination of cash, fame, and a bit of greed shaming—not to mention the threat of a legal battle and plenty of bad press if they tried to steal this from the world Jewish community were enough to turn even the greediest of claimants away.

One family that didn't make an appearance was the Conver family. In fact, Colette had no luck finding any of them. There were no records of Chloe, and Pierre-Antoine had taken a trip to Paris, pulling a magician's disappearing act. As for the hermit—he didn't return to his cave. Colette desperately wanted to find them. She knew the treasure belonged to them, that the treasure wasn't hers. She didn't want to be one of those people who bought something incredibly valuable from an old person for a ridiculously low price.

However, circumstances had made her that, not by intention but still—here she was. Her purpose in keeping the things she had snuck through customs was to ensure that she was able to give them back to the Conver family. The problem was, there were no Conver family members to be found, and from what she could tell, none of them had left any children behind. Of course, there are worse things than being burdened with a treasure trove.

Colette needed the time away from Morocco. She intended to go back, but for now, she needed to be back among her own people. She needed to get her head together, and she needed to have the treasure out of her riad. It was not good to have a basement full of treasure.

Almost immediately upon finding it, it had begun to make her crazy. She'd always laughed at those movies where friends end up killing each other over a big fortune they don't want to share. "There's enough for everyone to share," she'd always said. "Why in the world would they kill each other over it?"

But now she knew. Millions upon millions of dollars. It had made her lose her head. Not only had she wanted to protect it and keep it from everyone else, but it had made her suspicious and crazy. In the end, only one thing had saved her. Ahmed. The simple toothless smile of the Berber had shown her what was happening. As she realized what she had, she had expected that he was going to kill her over it. At the very least, she thought he would tell everyone, but in fact, he hadn't even tried to keep the gold coin she handed him. He handed it back to her and then, using body language, suggested that they lock up the room and go back upstairs before anyone wandered in.

His smile. It was genuine strength. He didn't care about money. Maybe all those women who had come to help with the house didn't care about money either. Maybe Simo wasn't in this for the money. Aziza? Well, maybe Colette was being too hard on the girl. It wasn't as if she had any claim to Yunis, hell, it wasn't even as if she actually wanted him. He had been a sort of grasping fantasy for a man to protect her. Something that she didn't need. Gold is oriented towards the East. That was what Chloe had told her. Love was to the West.

She wondered about that. Had Chloe been talking about her love of gold, kept locked up in a basement closet? Was she talking about how food and love were hopelessly intertwined—the stomach being the way to the heart and the pantry being the way to the stomach? Or was it something else—Colette didn't know. She might never know.

Being back in New York, Colette felt good about what she had accomplished. She felt good about her decisions. Before leaving Sanhaja, she'd asked Ahmed to take over the project of restoring the house. She'd arranged a large bank transfer to Wajaf, the big Moroccan bank and then told Simo that he would be working for Ahmed now. She gave both men a raise and left strict instructions to not let anyone move into or stay in the house besides the two of them. She would return when the house was fully restored. At that point, she would see what could be done about the hotel. For now, it was nice to be back in New York— and to be a star instead of just some crazy white lady who had bought an even crazier house.

Mooning

Chapter 25: Mooning

One of the things Colette couldn't figure out was how she had developed that crazy obsession over Yunis. He wasn't her type. She liked brainy guys with open minds and open hearts who when asked about God usually replied "Who?"

Before she left, she'd finally been able to sit down with Yunis, heart fluttering like a schoolgirl and within about a minute of the conversation, she didn't want to be near him. His English was decent, but his mind was soggy, maybe it was from all the baking. He'd talked about how much he loved God, how he was looking for a good Islamic woman, and about how life in Morocco gave him everything he wanted. "Those guys," he had motioned his arm expansively," out there, they all want to leave Morocco, but for me, everything I want is here."

It was at about that time that she'd realized just how little of what she wanted was in Morocco. Including Yunis. She wanted theater, fashion, arts, shopping, and bacon. Yes, bacon. She'd never before spent much time thinking about bacon or any other meat, but a few months in Morocco had driven her desire for bacon to a fever pitch. Maybe Yunis was just another sort of bacon, but it had been romance and flirting she was after, rather than salty smoked meat. Maybe that was the answer there.

In any event, she didn't miss him, and she didn't care if he and Aziza got married and had a hundred children. In fact, she didn't care about much besides this sudden desire to find Pierre-Antoine, Abraham, or the reportedly long-dead Chloe Conver. None of them had a listed telephone or address of permanent record, well except for the Hermit. Simo was watching for his return and promised to notify her right away when and if it happened. The whole situation had driven Colette to distraction.

There had been odd and mysterious occurrences each time she had met any of them. As she recalled each event, her skin had puckered into goosebumps. She would keep looking, and she would find them and return what was rightfully theirs, but the task seemed to be impossible. She delved into immigration records, birth certificates, and all of the genealogist's tools which finally led her to the Church of Latter-Day Saints, who have the largest collection of lineage tracing resources on the planet. She went to the New York Family History Center on Columbus Avenue. The ladies inside were helpful, and to her surprise, didn't try to convert her, though they did ask if she were a Mormon.

The search turned up something that she hadn't expected. By this point, this didn't surprise her. There was no record of the Conver family in Morocco, but she found that there was a wealthy Conver family from Marseille. They weren't Jewish, but the patriarch and founder of the family fortune was Nicholas Conver, just as the founding father of the Moroccan family had been named.

Conver had been a rich man, by any definition. There was little information that remained about him, there were several certain facts. Nicholas Conver had been the official engraver for the King of France and as such was a member of the diplomatic corps that had been sent to deal with the Sultans of Morocco. He had made the journey to Fez, which at that time was the Imperial capital and then had spent more than a year living there.

Interestingly, he was also the designer and engraver of one of the first European tarot decks. The tarot was a deck of cards used for a game in France at the time. It was steeped in mystery and used by fortune tellers from that time all the way to the present to tell fortunes. Some said that the tarot had origins older than the pyramids. Nicholas Conver was the original French tarot designer.

He had been sent to Fez, but there was no record of him or his family settling there. Today there were very few members of the Conver family to be found in Marseille, though she did find a small enclave that lived in a village near the town of Aix-en-Provence. That, however, was as far as she was able to follow that track. If she wanted to know more, she would have to go to France. Maybe once Riad Conver was completely restored, she would take on this quest.

Through immigration records, she found that Pierre-Antoine Conver had immigrated in 1947 from France, not from Morocco. The city of origin was listed as Marseilles. There was no record of a Chloe Conver immigrating to the United States. In fact, there was no record of a Chloe Conver anywhere—something that seemed impossible given that there were nearly 8 billion people in the world. A google search brought Colette to where it had all begun. Type: 'Chloe Conver' into Google, and you find ladies' handbags and exotic luxury designs, though the shop had disappeared from the street and from search results.

Colette didn't spend all of her time obsessing over the Conver family, the treasure, or thinking about her house in Morocco. She spent most of her time re-discovering just how much she had missed her beautiful city. Coming out of a Broadway show with Destiny, looking up at the sky, and seeing the full moon shining down between the valleys of massive towers.

"I love New York!" She shouted, much to the delight of the people around her who figured she was probably some tourist seeing the city for the first time. In her enthusiasm and amidst the laughter of Destiny and her other girlfriends, she spun around with her arms spread out and crashed right into some poor guy that was coming around the corner. She ended up knocking him and his pizza onto the ground with her on top of them both. It was a bacon pizza—she could smell it.

The Sun Rises

Chapter 26: The Sun Rises

Destiny and her friends pulled Colette off of the poor guy. His pizza was smooshed, but at least it was in a box and not smooshed on the two of them. Luckily it hadn't been raining, and the fall to the ground was easily brushed off. He was kind about the whole thing and laughed as they helped him up.

"It's not every day that I get mugged by a gang of beautiful women," he laughed. They all laughed with him. He wasn't terribly handsome, but he was pleasant looking, and his voice was particularly nice.

"I'm awfully sorry," Colette said. "I should pay more attention to what I'm doing."

Again, he laughed. "I'm rather glad that you weren't paying attention." He wiped away his curly black bangs from where they had fallen over his face. Colette, the jewelry designer, noticed that he had silver rings on every one of his fingers—including his thumb. He wore black trousers and a white jacket, which thankfully she hadn't ruined by knocking him in the gutter. As she brushed the back of it, she could feel the tightness of his muscles. He was in good shape.

"Let me make it up to you," she said. "Can I buy you a drink?"

"I thought that was supposed to be my line, but I accept. What's your name?"

"I'm Colette Samson," she told him, extending her hand.

"Lordy Lordy Colette Forty," he said, then seeing the scowl on her face, apologized. "Sorry, I bet you hate that. You're obviously much younger than forty." She forgave him instantly.

"I'm so pleased that we bumped into each other. I'm Nick. Nick Conver." He took her extended hand. His name caused her to take a step back and look into his face carefully. Was this some sort of a set up? Had he planned this? What was going on here—?

The look of surprise on his face as she pulled back wasn't faked, neither was the warmth of his voice. "Was it something I said?" It had to be a coincidence, which, she had learned by this point, was probably the last thing in the world it was.

"Let me buy you a drink, Nick. I won't take no for an answer." She moved back towards him and smiled. Her friends had fallen into their own conversations when they had seen that she was interested, and he looked like a likely candidate. That's the way friends were supposed to operate.

"In that case, the answer is yes. Right now, or would you rather meet later?" he asked.

"There's no time like the present," she said. "Come on, I know a little place right around the corner."

"What about your friends? Aren't they coming?" he spluttered, a bit surprised at being hijacked this way by a woman who had literally knocked him off his feet just minutes before. "Uh, what about my pizza?"

"Bring the pizza. I'll catch up with my friends later." There was a part of her that felt like a cougar grabbing this guy from the street and dragging him back to her den, but he was at least as old as she was and besides—she had a good reason to take him.

There were no shortages of places she could have taken him, but she chose to take him to the sky deck at the Broadway Bar. It wasn't the fanciest, wasn't the trendiest, or the chicest—but it was a place he could bring his pizza, and where they could talk without getting drowned out by the noise or the music. And besides, it was her guilty pleasure in New York City—nowhere else was there a view like this.

Finding a table and placing their drink orders (a gin fizz for her and a pastis for him) she got down to business.

"Nick, I hope you'll forgive me, but you've got an interesting name. Can you tell me about it?" There wasn't any point in beating around the bush.

"Sure, thanks. I've always thought it was kind of plain. It's a family name. My great grandfather times ten or so—he was Nicholas Conver. If you're into fortune telling or the occult, he was supposed to be the guy who made the fortune telling cards, the tarot. I mean, that's the story…," he trailed off as she stared into his face.

She could see it. She could see the family resemblance.

"Tell me about your parents," she said. The poor guy was getting the interrogation treatment and had to be feeling sorry to have accepted her invitation—actually, she had sort of demanded that too.

"There's not much to tell, Colette. My dad's Moroccan, and my mom is American. I was born in 1966. My parents divorced in 1979. My dad went back to Morocco, and my mom stayed here. I like football, I'm a Jets fan, I love the Yankees, I work in design, I'm single, not gay, I like watching action films, and I don't have any pets, but would like to have a dog if it weren't for the tiny apartment I live in. I'm Jewish, but I don't practice— it's just the blood." He was annoyed. Rightfully so. She was kind of being a demanding bitch.

"Nick. I'm sorry. Look, I should have said something instead of just interrogating you. I think I know your father. Is his name Pierre-Antoine? Do you have an aunt named Chloe?" It was all too perfect. It had to be. She knew it.

"No. Colette, I'm sorry. I think you've mistaken me for someone else. My dad's name is Abraham. I don't know anyone named Pierre-Antoine or Chloe. Thanks for the drink, but I think I'd better be going." He put a twenty on the table and stood up.

"Abraham? You've got to be fucking kidding me. Your dad is the fucking hermit of Sefrou?" Colette stood up too but at the mention of Sefrou, Nick sat back down.

"How did you know he was from Sefrou? I don't know about the hermit part, but yeah, my dad was—is from Sefrou. I haven't seen him since 1979 when he left. I've thought about looking for him—but wait a minute—do you know my dad?"

It was all a bit too perfect, but there it was. "Yeah, Nick. I wouldn't say that I know him, but I've met him. He's a very nice man. Did you know he's a Muslim?"

And that was how they started to get to know each other.

Judgement

Chapter 27: The Judgement

Over the next few months, Colette and Nick became an item. Before either of them knew what had happened and well before they had even thought about making any sort of announcement about their relationship, Colette's mother invited Nick's mother to her afternoon tea. To say it was a disaster would be an understatement.

Nick called his mother 'The Duchess' and when 'The Duchess' met 'The Empress' sparks flew—not the kind of sparks one might have expected though. The two took to each other like pasta and sauce, and soon the tea parties were being jointly planned by the two women, while all of the ladies in the court whispered together about the forthcoming engagement that the friendship of the two women obviously heralded.

Colette and Nick were among the last people to hear the announcement they were getting prepared to make. An acquaintance of Colette's had an aunt who was one of the court ladies, and she had told her niece about the 'Wedding of the Decade' that was coming when the Samson and Conver families were united in marital bliss.

"What?" Destiny was with them and nearly knocked Colette out over the news. "How dare you not tell me! You two are engaged? When did this happen?"

Nick had his face buried in his hands, and Colette stood up, taking a defensive posture.

"Destiny, I swear to god, this is the first time I've heard about this. Trust me, I'm more surprised than anyone. Nick, did you know about this?" Colette was worried. It wasn't that she didn't like him, in fact, she probably even loved him, but it had only been five months since she'd knocked him down and since that time, they had been dealing with a few other situations.

The Moroccan government had apparently been paying attention to the New York Times because suddenly they were in a fit to find out how $15 million in priceless cultural artifacts had been looted from the country under their noses. Colette was in the clear since she had officially donated everything to the Jewish Museum, and her 'personal' items had somehow not made it onto any manifests, but there was a firestorm between the Moroccan government and the Jewish Museum. Getting wind of it, the Israeli Museum and Jewish organizations around the world became involved and suddenly Riad Conver was being mentioned as a priceless historical artifact itself. A piece of Jewish heritage that needed to be preserved and protected.

Tour groups from Fez were now taking trips to Sefrou and Sanhaja to show the "Jewish" towns of Morocco. The groups were even coming up to the Cascade to see the riad where the fleeing Jews had hidden their valuables as they made their escape from Morocco.

That story became a political problem as the reality of the Jewish exodus from Morocco was a rather complex story. There was a long history of Judaism in Morocco, and there was nothing easy about it. There were times the Jews had been harassed and mistreated and other times when Moroccan Jews had really been the power behind the throne. Sefrou wasn't the only town that had a significant Jewish population before the exodus. Tangier, Tetuan, Essaouira, El Jadida, Chefshouen, and Fez all had large Jewish populations. The big problem was why had they all left so quickly. As late as 1971 there had still been at least 500 Jews living in Sefrou and Sanhaja, but as far as Colette had seen, there was no longer a single Jewish family there.

Conspiracy theories flew across the blogosphere as Israeli sources said that the Jews had been persecuted and driven from Morocco after the return of Mohammad V because of the support they had given to (and been given by) the French. There was certainly some truth to the accusation. On the other side, the Moroccan government claimed that Israeli intelligence agents had acted as provocateurs. They said it was planned violence and intentional rumor making that made things worse for the Moroccan Jewish community so they would immigrate to Israel. This accusation was also probably true. It was a tactic that was used elsewhere where there had been significant Jewish populations, especially if they weren't keen to leave their current homeland to populate the new Jewish state. The thing that no one actually knew was how much was truth and how much was made up on either side. This was the historical reality.

The entire situation moved to international court with the Moroccan government claiming that the entire treasure should be returned to Morocco to be housed in the Jewish Museum of Rabat, and the greater Jewish community arguing that the Jewish artifacts were safer in the hands of more established museum authorities outside of Morocco. At the end of the day, it was all about money. It was about money and the perceived profits that came from housing the treasure and bringing in tourism dollars. Arguments went on for months, and Colette was called to give depositions and testify, something she refused on the basis that she was a simple property owner who had turned the goods over to the highest authority she could find.

Nick, to her surprise, told her that she had done the right thing. He had a better claim to the treasure and the money it represented than anyone, but he said he didn't want any part of it. "Who knows who that belongs to Colette? It's not mine, that's for sure."

She had, at first, debated whether to tell Nick about the gold, books, and other things she had kept aside because she wasn't sure how to tell him, but on the first night that he came to her house, the night when she figured she was finally going to sleep with him (after nearly a month of dating), she figured there was no other way than to show him.

"Nick. I've got to show you something."

She opened the closet where she had stashed everything.

"I held these things back. I wanted to give them to your family." There were portraits, carpets, books filled with Arabic, English, and French, a small number of photographs, an old Gramophone, some records, and various items of clothing.

Nick was astounded. "Why didn't you tell me these things before?" He asked.

"I wasn't sure how to tell you. And with the whole 'Moroccan Hoard' thing going on, I wanted to be sure of you first, and well—there was this too." She pulled the iron banded box out from her closet. She went to her desk to get the keys, still on the giant ring. When she'd left Morocco, she'd left many of her personal things in the riad, but the keys had come with her.

"What is it?" He said as she opened it. This time, there was no mystery. It was very obvious that what was in the box was gold. A lot of very old, very valuable gold.

Nick laughed and then sat down. He kept laughing until the tears came into his eyes.

"Any word on my father yet?" he asked her.

She found the question odd given the circumstances but gave him the truth.

"No. I've asked Simo every time I've called. Your father still hasn't returned. I'll tell you as soon as I know but—Nick— why are you laughing?"

Nick wiped the tears from his eyes.

"When I was a little boy, my father used to tell me stories of our ancestors and of his homeland. I could always tell that he missed Morocco, that he wanted to go back. The stories were wonderful and filled with magic. Did you know that the evil wizard from 1001 Nights came from Morocco? Aladdan's palace was built in Morocco. So many wonderful stories. He used to tell me about the cave of Ali Baba, and how it was really an ancient Egyptian story."

"In my father's version, a French soldier falls in love with an Egyptian woman and follows her into a cave. There she reveals that she is a magic being, that she is willing to give herself to him, but that he can never possess her. The man agrees because he is so taken by her that he can only imagine death without her. The Djinni, she loves him, and she reveals that in order to speak to her, to contact her in her world, he only needs to use a set of cards that she gave to him. The tarot, they are called 'The Keys.' They allow for many things: contact between the Djinn world and ours, seeing the past, traveling to the future, and more. Then, this woman sends the man on his way with a box of Egyptian gold coins. Just like these."

Since returning from Morocco, Colette had been afraid to tell anyone about the single coin she'd received from Pierre-Antoine. She had worked it into a necklace that she made incorporating traditional Moroccan designs. She pulled the necklace from her desk, where she had been keeping it in a small velvet bag.

"Your uncle had some of them. When he sold me the house, he gave me one? Did I tell you about the strange things he did that day?"

"Colette, you don't understand. The French soldier was my ancestor, my namesake. This box of coins proves that the story was true. The gift of the Djinni and the deck of the Tarot, it's all real."

Colette could understand his shock, but she still wasn't the sort that would easily believe such things. Maybe it wasn't a coincidence, but certainly there wasn't any secret land of magic filled with Genies and Aladdin lamps. He'd come around. Still, it was an interesting story.

He didn't demand that she give him the things she had kept. He was most taken with the old books and would borrow a book or two. He brought them back before taking more. He enjoyed seeing the paintings and carpets, but he always put them back in the closet where she kept them. As for the gold, she'd asked him "What should we do with it?"

"It seems like it's okay there," he told her, motioning to it in the closet with his silver ringed hand. He was the strangest, most-sort-of-perfect man she had ever met.

The night that they heard about the judgment of the court of "The Duchess" and "Her Ladyship" they had already shared more than most couples who are engaged. They just hadn't shared that particular moment yet.

Nick raised his head from his hands and looked up to where Colette and Destiny were facing off. Taking a silver ring from his left pinky finger, he stood up from the table and got down on one knee.

"Colette," he whispered. "Will you marry me?" Their two mothers had foretold the future perfectly.

Colette never found out if they had been using Tarot cards. Destiny decided to believe their story, though she was never sure that Nick hadn't proposed a second time just to save their friendship.

As to the international courts and the problems between nations, as usually happens, money and reputation solved the problem. The Moroccan government was less concerned about the treasure than about the boon to tourism that it represented. Jewish tourism had become big business and the Moroccan government had been working hard to court Israeli, American, and British Jews to return to Morocco and buy property they had sold or left behind.

The moment that some smart lawyer accused the Moroccan government of trying to steal Jewish treasure, the PR people on the Moroccan side began to freak out. The last thing they wanted to do was alienate Jewish tourists. Luckily, several international Jewish organizations stepped up and suggested that Sefrou and Sanhaja should be declared a Jewish world heritage site. The old Medina had already been declared a UNESCO world heritage site, so it made sense. The Moroccan government wanted assurances that the restoration and preservation would be paid for by someone else. This solved the problem.

Riad Conver would become a Jewish Museum. The Moroccan treasure would remain with the Jewish Museum of New York, but Riad Conver would be developed into a tourist destination and roughly $30 million dollars was going to be spent on the preservation, restoration, and marketing of Sefrou and Sanhaja as a historic and cultural destination. The Moroccan government offered to buy the riad for $3 million U.S. dollars. She accepted, but only if they guaranteed a couple of conditions.

The World (Her Oyster)

Chapter 28: The World is Her Oyster

Her conditions brought no hesitation.

The first condition was that she and Nick be allowed to have their wedding in the riad, and that they and their descendants would be allowed to stay there for a month each year. They would oversee the rest of the restoration, act as governors, and be made members of a board of trustees that was set up to administer and take care of the foundation in Morocco.

Her second condition was that Ahmed be kept on as caretaker for life. He didn't have any children who were interested in taking over when he retired (or died) so there was no need to build a lifelong commitment.

She debated a third condition but, in the end, decided it was easier to tell them that the keys had been lost. She was keeping the keys. Locksmiths would create a new set, but these were for her and her descendants.

Everyone was just happy to have the whole thing out of court and any negative connotations out of the press.

The return to Morocco was again hectic, but this time it was because they were bringing far more with them than Colette had brought the first time. The treasure was left in Colette's New York closet where it would stay for nobody knew how long, but they had plenty of other luggage. One week before they left, it was time for Colette's birthday again. Hard to believe it had only been a year since she'd seen that billboard. This year, she knew she was safe from billboards because "Lordy Lordy, Colette Forty-One" sounded like a password or screen name. Even if it had happened, somehow, she was sure that she wouldn't mind as much as she had the year before.

The Duchess and The Empress both insisted on coming. The riad had been restored and upgraded to the point where it would be possible for them to be there. Electricity, showers, hot water, and Western flush toilets were available now, even though in a true restoration, that would never have been acceptable. Each of the ladies brought a mountain of luggage to help prepare for the wedding, and each of them had a mountain of ideas about how the wedding should go, even going so far as to have each written their own version of how the couple's vows should be read.

Simo had bought a second car and apparently Yunis had gotten into the driving business with him because the two of them were waiting among the many cigarette smoking drivers outside the arrival gate. This time, they drove directly to Sanhaja. Nick looked out the window, seeing for the first time the land of his heritage.

As they drove, he didn't speak, but the gentle squeeze he sometimes gave to Colette's hand told her that everything was alright. His father was still a no-show at his cave, but Colette was hopeful he would turn up. Nick didn't know what to think; he hadn't seen the old man for so long and was still hurt about being abandoned. They hadn't told his mother that Abraham was still (presumably) alive and living in Sefrou. It just hadn't been something that either of them had been willing to bring up with her.

The first person they met at Riad Conver was Ahmed who had gotten some serious dental work done. He smiled at Colette with a poorly fitted pair of false teeth that almost didn't fit in his mouth. She promised herself that fixing his teeth would be a top priority. He'd learned some new English too.

"Happy Hanukkah," he said when he met Nick. "Mazel Tov." He was becoming a regular New Yorker. Colette couldn't imagine what might have happened if he hadn't been with her that day she found the treasure. He had saved her from some awful greedy creature that had been growing in her. She grabbed him in a big hug and kissed his cheeks repeatedly. "Salaam a leycum you wonderful old Berber."

Ahmed was shy and respectful. He blushed and moved to help the two mothers who seemed to be terrified of him. He carted their luggage inside while Colette assured them that he was harmless and honest.

Aziza and Lala were waiting for them. The Moroccan aptitude for forgiveness is gigantic and though Aziza had been angry with Colette, it didn't show now. As for Colette, she still felt a little bit odd to be around Aziza—there was still a bit of something she didn't trust about her, but then she was embraced and welcomed back to her home by Jamila too.

If Aziza could forgive Jamila, the least she could do was forgive Aziza. The girl hadn't really done anything to her except maybe be a bad friend. Apparently, the sisters had healed their broken relationship, but there was no sight of Adil—some things could just never be put right. Aziza and Yunis were engaged. Simo was still single but told Colette about an old American woman he had met online. He was hopeful to marry and get a visa from her so he could move to America.

Riad Conver was coming along amazingly. Colette felt a twinge of regret at having sold it. The foundation had begun the work to bring the hotel back to life and put the tourist infrastructure back together around the cascade. When she saw this and realized how much work they had done and still needed to do, she felt no regret. It was best for the property, and it was not how she wanted to spend the rest of her life.

Sanhaja was a hotbed of activity as they prepared for the wedding, got everyone settled in, met with groups of tourists who had come to see the Moroccan treasure house, and worked with the rest of the trustees, the Jewish Museum, and the representative the Moroccan government had put in place to make sure that everything was done according to regulation (and that everyone got their proper baksheesh along the way.)

The days blurred as they finished the wedding plans, welcomed arriving guests, and prepared for any last-minute needs, so everything would be ready. They were going to have a big Moroccan wedding, but in the Jewish tradition.

"Did you know that Moroccan weddings and Jewish weddings are the same thing, Mr. Nick?" Colette had been afraid Simo would be jealous of Nick, but he had taken to him like a little kid to their older brother. "I bet you didn't know that our families used to be neighbors." Then whispering behind his hand "We all used to be Jews too, but don't worry, your Dad is a Muslim, so you are too. Hamdillah."

The more things changed, the more they stayed the same in Morocco. As to Sidi Ali Brahim, there was no word of him until the day before the wedding. Simo ran into the riad, red faced and out of breath.

"Miss Colette, Mister Nick. He's back. Sidi Ali, I mean, your father. He just got back. Come on!" And with that his round figure was out the door of the riad running for the car. Nick and Colette looked at each other, shrugged, and chased after him.

Back to the Fool

Chapter 29: Back to the Fool

It was a little awkward. They hadn't seen each other since Nick was thirteen. Back then his father had been a Jew. An American immigrant. A New York hippie with a mystical backstory. He'd left, disappeared, and moved into a cave.

He'd become a Muslim holy man. Some people said he was a saint. Some people said he was crazy.

Really, he was just Abraham Conver. Nick's dad.

As they walked up, he was unloading his luggage from the back of the little donkey he had apparently been riding. He didn't turn to look at them, but seemed to know exactly who they were.

"Lots of activity over there at the old homestead," he said. "You'd think they were planning a wedding or something."

Nick had been thinking about all the things he was going to say to his dad, all the anger he'd felt, all the questions he'd wanted to ask, but when the old man turned, there was a remembered twinkle in his eye, some little piece of magic that stopped everything Nick had been prepared with.

He pulled the basket off the donkey, picked up his blanket rolls, and moved to the open door. "Simo, will you make us some tea? I think we've got a few things to talk about." Abraham motioned toward the cave entrance.

They all moved inside the musty smelling cave and sat on the sheepskins, carpets and cushions.

"Dad?" It was all Nick could get out.

Abraham turned to him. "I'm sorry boy, it was your mother. If I stayed a minute longer, I think I would have killed her. She was driving me nuts."

"You could have written or visited."

"Yeah, I guess you're right. Hey, you know the story of the Buddha? He left his wife and son too."

"You're not the Buddha. Besides, the Buddha returned."

"That's true. Very true. But if I had been or if I'd have figured out the secrets of life—then I might have been, and then I would have come back. Anyway, I didn't. Sorry about that. I returned here, —even though I knew you all had come. The magic made me do it."

As much as he wanted to be angry, Nick just couldn't be. This was his dad. Exactly the same kooky person he remembered from the time he was a boy.

Colette had been thinking about something ever since Nick told her the story of the gold coins. She'd asked Nick, but he hadn't known the answer. She had to ask now.

"Abraham," she said. "Do you remember the story of the Egyptian Djinni and the French soldier you used to tell Nick?"

"Remember it? Of course, I remember it. It's my family's history. What do you think I'm some kind of an old fool?" He seemed much older than the last time she'd seen him—and a bit more addled.

"The Djinni," Colette said, "what was her name?"

"Well, I'm sure I told you that. I told you all about my sister and the cook, and I must have told you that."

"No, you didn't. What was her name?"

"Why, her name was Chloe, just like my sister's. In fact, it was she who my sister was named for. Family tradition. Eldest daughter is always named Chloe." Colette had guessed as much. She told herself she didn't believe, but she did. How could she not?

They tried to find out where he had been and what he had been doing for so long, but he was vague in his answers. "Oh, you know, these brotherhoods, they all like to argue and bicker with each other." Or "Lala Aisha probably wouldn't like it if I told you about that. What happens in Baboob stays in Baboob." And so, they were left telling him about their lives, which was probably what he wanted to hear about anyway.

They told him about the treasure, about the rooms under the fountain, about the way they had met and about the big hubbub that had broken out over the rights to the treasure. They told him about everything, and he listened, though it seemed like he already knew. Colette asked more questions about Pierre-Antoine and the Conver family, but he didn't seem willing to give any more answers than the ones she had found. Or he didn't want to share them. She told him about Aziza and the cook's journal and how the cook's son hadn't really died, but she held back from telling him that it was probably Chloe who had poisoned her and her new husband, the dashing Gerard. Overall, he just didn't seem as surprised as she would have expected—about anything.

"There's still plenty of secrets in that house. Don't you worry about that," he was interrupted by Simo bringing the tea, but he went on when the cups had been filled and distributed." Those secrets aren't going anywhere. Enough for all the generations yet to come too. Al-hamdillillah." That seemed like the right point to tell him about the wedding. He wasn't surprised.

"Didn't I tell you that your family history was all wrapped up with mine the moment you bought those keys?" They didn't tell him that the Duchess was there because it seemed like that might keep him from coming, but then, he probably knew that since he seemed to know everything else.

As they were leaving to head back to Riad Conver, he hit them with one more surprise.

"Well, well, well. My son's going to have a wedding. Just in time too, if you ask me," he said. "This one's going to start showing any time now and that would really get people talking—. So, what are you going to call our newest little fool?"

The End:The Beginning

The End (or The Beginning)

A few notes on the wedding…

Ahmed's new false teeth and advanced English vocabulary made him the star of the wedding, and while the bride and groom sat in state watching, they were surprised to find him in heavy demand from The Empress, the Duchess, and Lala—who, up to that point, hadn't really paid much attention to him at all.

Colette was indeed pregnant with a boy and gave birth eight months later. The grandmothers and Moroccans all agreed that it was amazing that the baby had been so well formed when he was born a month prematurely. Not wanting to saddle the boy with a name that was too Islamic, Jewish, or French—Colette and Nick agreed to name him Imhotep.

Colette decided to forego the feminist practice of hyphenating her name and changed her name to Conver. The truth was, she'd never liked the name Samson.

Abraham didn't want the gold. He and Nick agreed that Colette had found it, and she should keep it. She had plenty of money, so she kept the gold in her closet. Nick was more interested in the books and paintings. He told Colette they were filled with arcane information about the tarot, but she wasn't particularly interested.

After a couple of weeks, Nick and Abraham both figured out that they didn't have much more to say to each other, and at that point any regrets about the years apart were laid to rest. Abe couldn't hear very well, and Nick wasn't much of a talker. All the things he wanted to know about; his father told him he was too young to know.

Simo married his fifty-five-year-old girlfriend from Seattle and became the stepfather to a boy and girl who were each older than he was. He was a grandfather when he was barely old enough to be a father. Yunis and Aziza seemed to live happily-ever-after with him away driving most of the time, and her managing their family affairs.

The Jewish Heritage Museum and Hotel in Sanhaja were both a huge hit but caused one problem no one had expected. Every family that lived in a riad within 200-miles had soon ripped up their floors looking for hidden basement rooms. As of this moment, none of them have uncovered any treasure—at least not that they've said anything about.

Nick, Colette, and Imhotep moved back to New York City where Imhotep's sister Chloe was born, when he was two.

The wheel of fortune turns how it will. Did they all live happily ever after? Probably—after all, they had the keys.

www.ingramcontent.com/pod-product-compliance
Lightning Source LLC
Chambersburg PA
CBHW051333020726
47501CB00007B/2067